Kalorama

Carolyn Lyon Muehlhause

COVER PHOTOGRAPH: GEORGE C. LYON

Kalorama
©2006 Carolyn Lyon Muehlhause
Published by Wolf's Pond Press

All rights reserved. Printed in the United States. No part of this book beyond brief quotations may be reproduced without permission.

Library of Congress Control Number: 2006931432

Carolyn Lyon Muehlhause, 1923 -

ISBN 978-0-9702249-2-7
Washington D.C. – Depression era – Fiction. 1. Title

Book design by Kelly Prelipp Lojk
Cover photograph by George C. Lyon

Manufactured in the United States of America

FOR MY FAMILY

ACKNOWLEDGMENTS

First and foremost, I thank Laurel Goldman, master teacher, mentor, and dear friend, for her steadfast and wise council. I also thank the members of Laurel's Thursday Morning Class: Jackie Ariail, Billie Hinton, James Ingram, Sonia Johnson, Willie Mason, A. J. Mayhew, Mary Michael, Lucinda Paris, Christina Askounis Pogoloff, Betty Reigot, Eve Rizzo, and Maureen Sladen.

In addition, all the people listed below have, in diverse ways, assisted in getting Kalorama into print: Pamela Muehlhause Cleary (formerly Garside), Georgann Eubanks, Lee Hansen, Nan Kwock, Elena Rosario Loomis*, Mr. and Mrs. George C. Lyon and daughter*, Shirley Martin, Ruth Messenger, Carl Oliver Muehlhause, Virginia O' Connell, Maria V. Delgado-Rodas*, Edna Ross, Sheryl and Ron Williams, and Ted and Shirley Wood.

* Resided at Kalorama

PREFACE

In the early years of the twentieth century, a rose brick mansion graced the corner of 1867 Kalorama Road, Washington, D.C. Designed by Stanford White, America's celebrated architect, the beautiful residence welcomed visitors to a neighborhood of embassies, legations, and estates. Who would have guessed that, only a few years later, a jealous husband would murder Stanford White? Or that the stock market crash of 1929 would usher in the Great Depression? By the 1930s, the rose brick mansion had become a boardinghouse.

Memories keep alive that place and time. Five of us (see acknowledgments*) lived in the boardinghouse. A good many of those listed have memories of the decade known as Hard Times. The setting of my novel is 1935. The characters are imaginary. No actual person, living or dead, plays a part in this fictitious story.

JANUARY 1935

1

Nels Weigmann pulled the Rickenbacher close to the curb and let the engine idle while he lit an Old Gold. Twice he'd circled the block and parked across the street from his home. By now Mid must have spotted the car. She'd be ready for him—all tuned up for another shouting match. Damned if he felt up to it.

He shifted gears and headed down Kalorama Road. Along both sides were huge houses with well-tended lawns. He braked in front of his favorite. Although at least a decade older, it

resembled his own place, a Georgian colonial designed by Stanford White. The fanlight above the entrance caught his eye, but this was not the time to enjoy it. He needed to take some pills to dull the throbbing in his bum leg. And he needed something—maybe a prairie oyster—for his hangover.

He parked outside 1867 Kalorama Road. Twin flights of brick steps curved up to the front door. Even after six years as owner and manager, he still felt in awe of the mansion—and what they'd managed to do with it. They'd created Kalorama, a unique boardinghouse. At least, it had no equal in Washington, D.C.

Holding a box of candy, he limped toward the house. Sunlight warmed its rose-colored bricks, but the evergreen shrubs looked frozen. He grasped the wrought iron railing and climbed a couple of steps. At least a dozen more lay ahead.

"Oh hell!" Back again on the brick path, he headed toward the short flight leading down to the English basement. Without doubt, Mid was there, busy with something she had to do in the dining hall or kitchen. "Smile, old buddy," he told himself. "It's only Mid. Not Fritzie Boy."

In a strong baritone, Nels sang as he unlocked the door,

"Last night, in the pale moonlight
I saw you, I saw you
You were mending your barbed wire

KALORAMA

When we opened rapid fire.
If you want to see your father
in the Fatherland,
Keep your head down,
BANG!
Fritzie Boy."

At the first sound of a car stopping, Mid ran from the kitchen into the adjoining entry hall. Its windows afforded a better view of Kalorama Road.

"Watched pots never boil," her father called after her. He continued to grate cabbage—more than enough slaw for the family and their paying guests.

Back at the counter, Mid stirred codfish into mashed potatoes. "It was my hubby all right."

"Sure it was Nels?"

"Who else around here drives a Rickenbacher?"

He carried the pail of salad into the pantry. As soon as he returned to the kitchen, he poured coffee into two cups. "Java's ready. Get it while it's hot!"

They sat at a round table in the center of the large kitchen. Some distance away stood a line of porcelain sinks topped by tall windows. Wrought iron grilles obscured the view, but both father and daughter could see the legs of anyone approaching the house.

"He drove away. Why doesn't he come home?" she asked.

"Maybe he's not in the mood to dodge dirty dishes." His cup clicked sharply against the saucer. "Didn't you realize what you were doing? The new china cost us thirty dollars."

Mid flushed to the roots of her titian-red hair. It was close to the color of her father's hair, now that his close-cropped red curls held threads of white. Mid had inherited his hazel eyes as well. Her sturdy, buxom body was like her mother's. Photographs were Mid's only way of knowing her mother, who had died of tuberculosis.

Bill Norris took note of his daughter's embarrassment. "You knew that Nels drank before you married him. My God, Mid, for twelve years you've tried to change him. Why not admit you can't? It would be different if he hurt you or the kid, but Nels never shows up until he's cold sober. Still you put all of us through hell every time he goes off on a toot."

Mid carried her cup of coffee to a counter already spread with waxed paper. It was soon covered with nearly identical codfish balls. "His leg's been acting up again," she said. "He doesn't tell me—you know how close-mouthed he is about all that—but I heard him making an appointment at Walter Reed. If they have to scrape the bone again, he'll be laid up for months. He never even phoned me."

Bill had assembled the ingredients for cornbread. With the ease that comes from many years of practice, he made the batter. "How about peas with the codfish balls? We're rich in canned peas."

"Good idea. I'll fancy them up with a cream sauce. Last night I made lemon meringue pies."

"I saw them in the icebox. Beauties! Nobody makes better pies than you do, Mid." He took several hot pans from the oven and began to butter and fill them with the cornbread batter. "I also happened to notice that the last of the rice pudding's gone." He set the pans into the oven.

"I blew the diet at about four this morning."

Bill gave his daughter an affectionate grin.

She tried to smile back. "I'm sorry about breaking all those dishes. It doesn't do a bit of good to fight with Nels. All it does is scare Nora."

As if she'd heard her name spoken, the seven-year old ran into the kitchen. "Mrs. Flagglar has a nose cold. She wants Corinna to bring a tray." Nora's small, heart-shaped face glowed with the excitement of delivering the message.

The maid had followed Nora into the kitchen. "She be asking for tea and toast. You want for me to fix it?"

"You fill the teapot," Mid said. "I'll make toast—I know just how she likes it. How sick is she? Will she need a dinner tray?"

Nora and Corinna looked at each other. "Her face is real white—as white as her hair," Nora said.

"Her nose is as pink as her wallpaper."

Bill chuckled. "Letty Flagglar would never wear a pink nose to dinner."

Nora watched as her mother prepared thin, crisp slices of toast and poured honey into a small pitcher. "Yummy! Can I have some, too?"

"You've had your lunch."

Nora joined her grandfather at the kitchen table and whispered in his ear.

Bill looked up from his newspaper. "You heard what your mother said."

Mid handed the tray to Corinna. "Tell Mrs. Flagglar that we'll send a dinner tray at seven." She shook her finger at Nora. "Miss Eleanora, go play in your room. No skating. It's going to rain."

Nora did not go upstairs. In the hall she sat on the bottom step of the polished oak staircase and picked at the scabs on her knees. The only thing she wanted to do was skate, but Momma never let her play outdoors in falling weather. What else was there to do? With her eyes closed, she imagined that Daddy Bill had made a big pancake for her. It was shaped like a bunny with very long, crispy ears. She could almost smell the warm butter and maypolene syrup.

"Girl, you be right smack in my way," Corinna said. Steadying the tray, she squeezed past Nora and hurried up the stairs. Nora got up and followed Corinna to the entrance hall. Highbacked chairs lined the walls of the room. A game of

musical chairs? Singing her favorite songs would be nice, but the real fun was in the surprises. She'd always know when to run to the nearest chair.

Corinna rested the tray on the hall table. "Nora, your momma always be touchy when your daddy's away. You got no call to feel bad. Besides, this be Saturday. I been expecting to walk you to the movie show."

"But the Ambassador doesn't open 'til one. What can I do now?"

"If I was you, seem like I could think of something." A dimple appeared in the left cheek of Corinna's light brown face. "Mights be I'd tend to them knees." She picked up the tray and headed for a flight of stairs curving up to the second floor.

Nora looked around the big, square hall. One pair of closed doors led to Col. Smith's suite, but she wasn't allowed to bother him. Besides, he liked to pinch her cheeks, and it always hurt when he did. The colonel was not one of her favorite grown-ups. The other doors led to the drawing room.

"You may not go into the drawing room," Momma had told her. "Not unless Aunt Bobbie or another adult is with you." Aunt Bobbie wasn't really her aunt. She was her friend and piano teacher, but she was never home on Saturdays.

Nora slid back one of the heavy walnut doors— just enough to squeeze through the opening— then closed the door behind her. Her heart was

beating fast. Remembering the burn of Momma's hairbrush sent shivers down her legs. She looked around the long, sunny room.

Three mostly red carpets lay on the polished floor. Aunt Bobbie liked them a lot. She called them the Persian Trees of Life. A crystal chandelier hung above the middle of each one. Sometimes Corinna had to shine all their crystals. She'd tear old towels into rags and drop them into a bucket of hot water and ammonia. Corinna never let anybody help her with the washing.

Sunlight streamed into the room. The grand piano stood near the bay window in the middle of the long wall. Nora wanted to run her fingers up and down the keys, but she was afraid somebody might hear the music. Also, Young Mozart seemed to be watching her. There wasn't much of him— just his white marble head with long curls, his neck, and some of his shoulders. He perched on top of a black marble pillar in the center of the bay. Green plants stood all around him.

Nora tiptoed past the piano to the marble fireplace. Flanked by tall windows with dark red velvet draperies, it occupied most of the back wall. On its mantel stood a white and gold china clock from France. Every once in a while the clock played bars of Mozart's music. One day Aunt Bobbie had told her that she admired their ragged robins. "I don't see any robins!" Nora had complained. That's when she found out that "ragged

robin" meant the pretty flowers painted on the vases.

She turned and ran down the long room to her favorite sofa. It faced windows overlooking Kalorama Road. She jumped into the down-filled center cushion. Across from her were two armchairs upholstered like the sofa. The pattern showed people with white hair who wore fancy costumes. They were having a tea party, and a little white poodle was begging for cookies.

In the space between the two front windows stood a marble-topped table with a very big vase on top of it. Corinna always called it The Vahze. On its shiny black sides goldleaf people in nightshirts were eating grapes and dancing. Aunt Bobbie thought that the people were Greeks.

Nora stared at the enormous vase. Could something be hidden inside it? She climbed up on a highbacked chair and reached down the neck. No sooner had she found a metal seal, than strong hands lifted her down.

"My stars, Nora! What was you fixin' to do?"

When Nora started to answer, Corinna interrupted her. "Your momma say you is to put them rompers in the laundry bag. You is to put on your pongee movie clothes." She frowned and pointed to the open doorway.

A draft was making the chandeliers sway slightly and chime. Sunlight passing through the crystals cast hundreds of darts of red, amber, green, and

violet onto the ceiling and walls. Nora listened and watched until Corinna closed the doors.

Out of the corner of her eye, Mid saw her husband limp across the kitchen and put a box of candy on the table. He placed his gloves, fedora, overcoat, and scarf on a chair.

She felt his eyes on her. God help me, she thought, I'm going to yell at him. If I don't do something, I'll explode! She pressed her body hard against the counter and finished the job of cutting sheet cake into petit fours. The radio story was nearing its end, but she couldn't follow it.

She snapped off the radio and motioned toward the candy. "Is that supposed to make up for last night?"

After a pause he said, "I guess it's a stab in that direction."

She looked straight into his eyes. Brown eyes under peaked eyebrows were Nels' best feature. She had fallen in love with those eyes, and his too-big nose, and quick smile. At their first meeting she'd felt drawn to him, a veteran still in uniform. And on crutches. She'd given him her desk on the aisle. After that, they'd been seatmates for quite a few college courses.

Mid pulled off the tea towel she'd used as a kerchief and ran her fingers through her curly bangs.

He's waiting for me to start something, she thought.

The kitchen was quiet except for the sound of the percolator. He said, "I could stand some coffee. How about you?"

"Not now." But she sat down at the table. Soon he took the chair across from her. On the table between them were the percolator and two pounds of Martha Washington's deluxe assortment.

She gave a short laugh. "How did this little toot get started?"

Nels steadied his cup with both hands, then sipped his black coffee.

With trembling hands she twisted the towel on her lap. "You must have had a swell time. You couldn't waste one minute of it to phone me. "

He slipped the satin ribbon off the candy box, took off the lid, and passed the candy to her. "The doctor won't operate—at least, not now. Not much to tell you."

"You could have told me last night. I'd have had less to worry about."

He poured another cup of coffee. "Sorry you worried, Mid. The poker game went on most of the night—a lucky one for me. Twenty clams ahead!"

"Poker on Friday night?"

"Pete Munden happened to be at the hospital. We got to chewing the rag and ended up at his flat.

A few highballs, some buddies dropped by—you know how it goes." Nels washed down two pills with a gulp of coffee. "Pain killers—or so they're called." When he opened a fresh pack of cigarettes, he offered her a smoke.

"I've got to frost the petit fours. Boarders' bridge night, remember?" She went to pour vanilla glaze over the cakes, then filled a pastry bag with icing.

Nels walked to the window overlooking the rose garden. The plants had a silver cast, and the sky looked lead-gray. "It's going to snow," he said. "Where is everybody?"

"Nora's at the movies. Pop's working in Mrs. Flagglar's bathroom. I declare, I can't imagine what she does to that water closet."

"Oh, come on, Mid! There's not one damn thing wrong with that toilet. Letty's pushing seventy, but she still likes to flirt. What's Corinna doing?"

"Until she goes for Nora, she's polishing furniture—mainly in the drawing room." Mid squeezed ruffles of chocolate butter cream on the last of the cakes. "Can you eat? Fish chowder's on the stove."

He filled a bowl and carried it to the table. Following, Mid handed him a box of crackers. "I caught Nora in the hedgerow again this morning. Freezing weather, but she was outside without her coat. No matter what I say, she thinks she has to watch when Philip Ayres beats his dog."

"Damn his hide! I'm going to have to talk with that bird!"

"I've already tried that. He told me to mind my own business. He said Pixie can't go on messing up his cellar."

"Why doesn't he get a doghouse?"

"That tightfisted guy?"

Nels took a long drag on his cigarette. "Let's give Nora a puppy! She'll forget all about Ayres' mutt."

"We've already settled that. If Nora has a pet, some of the boarders will want pets. No pets!" Mid's voice had an edge to it.

"Okay, no pets. But this early morning vigil's got to stop. There's something damned unhealthy about it." He dropped his cigarette butt in his empty bowl. "The kid's too lonely. We should have thumbed our noses at hard times and given her a little brother."

Ignoring the remark, Mid looked out the window. "It's snowing, and it's sticking, too!" She watched as the flakes blanketed the yard. "Want some lemon pie?"

"No, I'll just finish my coffee." He reached for the box of candy.

After he'd found his favorite caramels, Mid chose a cup of Jordan almonds. "Pop thinks we ought to let the Haskells come. He says that the Haskell kid is a godsend. What do you think?"

"They get my vote. I never did buy your regulation against children. The Haskell kid's probably spoiled rotten, but she's a pretty little thing. I can't say I go for her snooty mother."

"Lois Haskell's no snob. She's a Bostonian—she can't help her accent. Pop thinks she's a very unhappy woman." Mid selected a pink almond candy.

"What makes him say that?"

"Apparently she can't get used to being divorced. I wonder if she's found another place. Why not find out? The number's on her calling card—under the telephone."

He limped to a small desk and moved aside the embroidered screen concealing the telephone. After a brief chat about the weather with the telephone operator, he placed the call. "Mrs. Haskell? Nelson Weigmann here. Have you decided? Yes, breakfast and dinner are included. No, we don't provide luncheon. So, will you and your pretty little daughter be coming to Kalorama?"

He continued to talk, and Mid listened. She liked the sound of his deep voice and the way he had of befriending everybody.

As he hooked up the receiver, he said, "It's in the bag! She'll let us know when to expect them." He gave her a triumphant grin.

Mid smiled back. She turned on the radio and cut the crust from a large loaf of bread. Dividing the loaf in four long slices, she felt Nels' lips against her ear.

Nels pulled out one of her tortoise shell hairpins and used it to tuck several loose tendrils into her chignon. He kissed her other ear. She made a

kissing sound, but kept to the job of spreading cream cheese and sprinkling chopped nuts. She didn't notice when he collected his things and left the kitchen.

The Haskells were taking Second Floor South, an expensive suite. Nora would have a playmate close to her own age. As Mid sliced ribbon sandwiches, she sang along with the radio,

"Just around the corner
There's a rainbow in the sky,
So let's have another cup of coffee,
And let's have another piece of pie!"

2

"Are you Nora?" Nora dropped her bookbag on the hall table. "That's my nickname. My real name is Eleanora Weigmann. Who are you?"

"Flo. Florence Haskell. I'm going to live here."

Nora smiled at her. Flo looked nice—small and pretty with silky blond hair. "Daddy told me that you were coming. How old are you?"

Flo held up one plump hand and one extra finger. "But I'll be seven in August."

"You can't catch up to me. I'll be eight in April."

"Will you play with me?"

"Sure, but first I have to put on my rompers. I'm not allowed to play in school clothes."

Nora took another look at Flo's blue silk sash

and patent leather shoes. "Not at school today?"

"I start tomorrow. I'll be in Miss Deming's room."

Nora wrinkled her nose and turned down the corners of her mouth. "Next year you'll get Mrs. Lowe. She's swell!" Nora picked up her bookbag and motioned for Flo to follow.

They went past the entrance hall to the back hall that led to the Weigmanns' bedrooms. The former dining room had become the master bedroom and sitting room. The former breakfast room now belonged to Nora. She led the way through her parents' suite to her own bedroom and its door to the hall. The back stairs were nearby. "This is the way to the dining hall," she told Flo, then yelled down the stairwell. "Momma, I'm home!"

From below came Corinna's voice. "Ain't no call to holler. Your momma already know."

The children went back to Nora's room. It had four tall windows, and built-in corner cupboards held books, toys, games, and dolls.

Flo blinked. "Your room's brighter than mine."

"It's the yellow wallpaper. And the exposure. Every room on this side of the house has southern exposure." Nora had heard her father say it so many times. As fast as she could, she changed her clothes. "How do you like my rompers? Momma makes 'em out of Daddy's old shirts. I have to wear these 'til they don't fit anymore."

Flo looked at the white broadcloth rompers

with bright red buttons down the front. "I wish I had rompers. I don't have clothes to play in."

"What'll we play?"

Flo was not as pretty when she smiled. She had lost two front teeth in her upper jaw. "Hide and seek?"

Nora felt doubtful. "I'm not sure where we could do it." She led the way back to the entrance hall.

"Can we hide in there?" Flo pointed to a pair of pocket doors.

"That's the drawing room. When it's four o'clock Corinna opens the doors. But we can't play in there. We can't play in there either." Nora pointed to pocket doors across the hall.

"Why not?"

"That's where the colonel lives."

"Who's he?"

"Col. Smith. He was a brave soldier who got hurt in the war. One of his arms is real tiny. He wears a black sock on it."

Flo's smile disappeared. "What about my floor?"

They ran to the divided staircase leading to the second floor. Each raced up a different flight of curving stairs. "I won!" Flo shouted when she reached the top.

Nora had let her new friend win the race, but she wouldn't tell Flo—or anyone else that secret. "Look over the railing, Flo." The girls peered down at the entrance hall. Then they took note of the closed doors of the three suites on the second floor.

"Can we play in your rooms?" Nora asked.

Flo shook her head. "Mama's taking her nap. She has to rest every afternoon."

"I expect she's tired from the trip. Momma told me you came on the train. From Boston."

"Daddy's still there. So's my nanna." Flo sighed. "But we didn't come today. We've been visiting Uncle Earl. He lives in Arlington."

"Why don't you stay at his house?"

"Because of Aunt Lillian." Flo looked around before she whispered, "Mama doesn't like her very much." She pointed to the double doors of the center suite. "Who lives there?"

"Mrs. Flagglar. She has shiny white hair, and she smells like flowers—even sweeter than our rose garden. One time she gave me a back scratcher that she got in Japan. But she's not home. When she's home, her doors are open."

Flo pointed to the suite in the northwest corner. "Who's in that one?"

"The Telfords went to live with their daughter. The new boarders aren't here yet. Let's go up to Third. I can show you where Aunt Bobbie lives. She's my best friend." Nora paused. "Aunt Bobbie is my best grown-up friend. But she won't be home until dinner time because she works for the government."

Nora and Flo tapped on Roberta McElroy's door. To their surprise, she opened it. She was wrapping a towel around her wet, gray hair.

"Hello, Nora! Who's this?"

"Her name's Florence Haskell. Flo lives on Second South."

"A playmate! That will be nice for both of you."

The children followed Aunt Bobbie into her sunny corner room. Nora led the way to a steamer trunk, and when she sat on its curved lid, Flo scrambled up beside her.

"This trunk's full of music," Nora told her.

Flo moved forward so that her feet could touch the floor.

Bobbie smiled. "No brass bands in there, Flo. Nora means sheet music—you know, writing that tells me what to play on the piano."

"Is that your piano downstairs?"

"It belongs to Nora's parents, but I use it every day. I'm teaching Nora how to play. Would you like piano lessons?"

"If Mama lets me." Flo was watching the way Aunt Bobbie set her hair. Looking in her vanity mirror, Bobbie positioned long, reddish-brown combs. Soon there were neat rows of them, the teeth of one comb lacing the teeth of another. Aunt Bobbie secured them with big orange rubber bands and a brown net. "Sometimes I have to sleep with my hair tied up in rags," Flo said.

"Not me," Nora said. "Momma never curls my hair. She just cuts it short so my bangs are neat and my ear lobes show." She went to help Aunt Bobbie drop the rest of the combs into a

drawstring bag. "How come you're home so early, Aunt Bobbie?"

"While I was eating my lunch, I swallowed the filling in a tooth. I had to go to my dentist. After that, I took some fruit to my brother. Lester's in the hospital." Seeing the look of concern on Flo's face, Bobbie added, "He's been in the hospital quite awhile, but he's doing as well as can be expected. That's his picture on my dresser. Of course, he's older now. A lot older." She indicated a silver frame containing the photograph of a young man.

The girls went to take a closer look at Lester. Nora liked his smile and deep-set blue eyes. "He looked like you, Aunt Bobbie."

"He still does," Bobbie said. She sat down in her cretonne-covered easy chair, lit a cigarette, and watched as the girls studied her other pictures. A dozen or more photographs of a large white farmhouse and country scenes decorated the blue walls. "That house is where my brother and I grew up," she said. When she got near the end of her Lucky Strike, she used a wire hairpin to hold it.

Someone came to the door. "Sorry to disturb you, Miss McElroy," Corinna said, "but this be Hoover day. I gots to pass over your carpets."

"Of course, Corinna. Girls, you'll have to excuse us. So long until dinner time!" Bobbie gave them smiles and hugs.

KALORAMA

Nora and Flo looked at the pale gold wallpaper and green carpet runner of the hall. At each end of the hall, an open door revealed a white bathroom. They took turns tapping on bedroom doors. No one answered.

"Upstairs?" Flo asked.

"I'm not allowed on Fourth."

"Why not?"

"The college boys live there. They have to study, and I must not 'sturb them."

Near the end of the hall, a bedroom door was ajar.

"Who lives there?" Flo asked.

"Miss Esther, and she's real nice. She teaches the big kids." Nora called through the opening, "Miss Esther, can we come in?" Nobody answered. Nora gave the door a firm nudge. Facing them was a curio cabinet filled with dolls.

Flo ran across the room to the cabinet. "Oh, look at the boy in the red and yellow pajamas!"

"She got him in China. His head's made of porcelain. See the lady with the tall comb in her hair? She came from Spain. Don't you just love her lace dress? Every summer, Miss Esther goes somewhere. She always gets a doll for her collection."

Nora was about to open the glass door when something clattered to the floor. Corinna propped up the dust mop and lifted the carpet sweeper into the room. "You two hasn't ought to be in here.

Not without Miss Lovell. I seen her downstairs with Nora's momma."

"But Miss Esther and I play dolls all the time, and we look at her memory books." Nora pointed to a bookcase stuffed with scrapbooks. "She collects postcards, and she takes snapshots with her Brownie camera. That's so she can remember where she got her dolls."

"Maybe so. Now I gots my work to do. Scoot!"

The girls went down to Second Floor, but found nothing to interest them. Except for white wainscoting and storage closets instead of bathrooms, the hall resembled the one above. They looked over the railing at the entrance hall.

"Do you know how to play musical chairs?" Nora asked.

Flo shook her head.

"I'll teach you!"

Taking opposite sides of the divided staircase, the girls raced downstairs. This time, Nora won.

"Mid, can you help me?" Standing in the doorway to the kitchen was a tall, slender woman with a worried expression.

Mid dropped a pared potato into a large pot of salted water. "Esther? What's wrong?"

"I feel awful. Lots of students are out with the grippe, and everybody else seems to have a cold.

The school nurse thinks I'm coming down with something. She told me to take an aspirin and drink hot lemonade."

"Sit down while I fill the thermos." On her way to the pantry, Mid lit the gas under the kettle. She came back with two lemons. "Esther, I'm no nurse, but I'd advise you to stay in bed tomorrow. Take a day of sick leave."

"I can't!" It was a muffled wail. Esther had buried her face in her folded arms on the table. Only her wavy, light brown hair showed.

"Why can't you?"

Esther sat up. Her brown eyes were wet. "Sick leave? It would take me a week to get the kids in line again."

"Isn't Western High a college-prep school? I thought those kids were always in line."

"I guess I never told you. At the last minute, somebody else got the position at Western. The only other opening was tenth grade English at Ben Franklin. It takes me almost an hour to get there. Anacostia."

"Anacostia? I thought that section had gone colored."

"The students are white, but a good many don't speak English at home. It's a vocational school." Esther wiped her eyes and blew her nose.

Mid wrapped a tea towel around a thermos bottle and handed it to Esther. "What about dinner tonight? Corinna could take up a tray."

"Yes, thanks, Mid. Lemonade, my hot water bottle, and bed. I'll sweat it out today and be fighting-fit tomorrow."

"I hope you're right," Mid walked as far as the stairs with her. Esther had always taught college students. Why would she go to a vocational school in Anacostia?

KALORAMA

3

Esther's alarm clock forced her out of her warm bed. Her throat was still sore. She hurried into her robe and slippers, turned on a light, and silenced the clock. With her bag of toiletries and a towel, she went down the hall to the bathroom. As usual, she was the first to claim it. The other early riser on Third Floor was Walter Buchanan, who seldom got up before six. They'd exchanged few words—just enough to make her want to get better acquainted with him. Already she knew that the tall, gray-eyed gentleman was a traveling salesman. Recently divorced.

"What'll I wear today?" She couldn't decide until she looked into her chifferobe. Her new Irish woolens filled a third of the space. Why save them for Sunday-best? She took out her nicest tweed

outfit. Custom-tailored, the suit had a matching cape and hat. Everyone who'd seen it had admired the muted autumn colors of the tweed. Against her cheek, the fabric felt silken soft. Its faint scent reminded her of an Irish meadow filled with wildflowers.

While she dressed, she thought about her last vacation. The literary tour of Ireland had wiped out her savings, but every penny had been well spent. She'd visited places made famous by the world's poets. Her favorite was Innisfree, the beautiful lake isle so loved by Yeats. Next time, I'll stay longer, she promised herself. And go with a friend. Touring with strangers isn't as much fun as it used to be.

When she walked into the main office at Franklin, Principal Howard Newton greeted her. He looked well-scrubbed and ill clad. The former football coach always seemed to wear an unbuttoned three-piece suit in need of a press.

She smiled and said, "Good morning," in a voice that did not sound like hers.

"You're free second period, aren't you?" he asked.

"They need me in the book room. My supplemental texts finally came."

He seemed to be studying her outfit. "Our chat won't take long. I'll expect you at the beginning of the period." He gave her what looked like an approving smile, then took a shortcut through the

maze of clerks, desks, and filing cabinets and disappeared behind the back door to his private office.

Less than two hours later, Esther was staring at Mr. Newton across his cluttered desktop. "I don't understand what you mean," she said. He'd seemed unable to get to the point. Could he be planning to let her go? Didn't he realize how much she needed this job?

"You don't want to understand." He glanced at his wristwatch.

She tried to swallow. Instead, her throat tightened. "May I tell you why I came to Franklin?" Her voice sounded hoarse. For years she'd received compliments on her speaking voice, especially the musical quality of her laughter. At his nod she spoke, but her voice kept breaking.

"This is my first experience with adolescents. I've spent eighteen years with college students. Rather poor financial benefits, of course, but I found the work very rewarding. I've always assumed that my inheritance would take care of me in old age." She gave him a wry smile. "Last March I buried my father. He left me nothing but a few unpaid bills."

Newton ran his fingers through his short, gray-brown hair. Then he leaned forward and looked directly into her eyes. "Esther, I understand your situation. A good many of our women teachers are overqualified. They've come to the public schools

because they need tenure. They don't all get it. Unless things improve, I will not recommend you for tenure. We're getting too many complaints."

"Complaints about me?" She felt a sharp stinging in her eyes.

"Kids are begging for transfers. Yesterday, several from your last class came to see me. What's going on?"

"Period Six is Remedial English. Forty-two pupils—mostly tenth graders, but several are older." She handed him a leather portfolio. "My plans for this week."

He snapped on his desk lamp and began to examine the neatly typed sheets. As the minutes passed, Esther tried to rub her sore throat, but her cold hands only made it feel worse. She fingered the soft, even waves in her hair.

I must not stare at him, she thought. She rotated her chair so that she faced the window. In front of a tall privet hedge were racks filled with the faculty's bicycles. How she'd enjoy going to work that way!

She blinked away tears. Think about something else, she told herself. Saturday morning. Unless the weather got awful, she'd ride her bike. She needed exercise. And it would be fun to explore an unfamiliar neighborhood—maybe discover an interesting shop. That was how she'd found the beauty parlor. At last, someone with talent marcelled her hair. The place would soon be outfitted to give the

Croquinole. Hair got attached to electric cords dangling from the ceiling. It took only a few minutes to get one's hair permanently curled. Esther closed her eyes and pictured herself with curls. No, she preferred waves. The Ann Harding look.

With a loud click, Newton turned off his lamp. "You know your stuff—no doubt about it. The problem is, our youngsters aren't comfortable with lessons like these. They'd be fine for a college-prep school, but they're inappropriate for Franklin." He walked over to her and returned the portfolio. "Esther, the kids aren't with you. You must find a way to win them over. Then you'll be able to teach them. Are you willing to try?"

She nodded, close to tears again, and followed him to the outer office.

"Your department chairman can help you," he said. "You'll find a message in your mailbox. Tom Branscom's been in this game for years. With some pointers from Tom, you'll soon be hitting the basket every time." He left her near the teachers' mailboxes.

Without stopping to pick up her messages, Esther raced to the women's lavatory. No one else was there. She clung to the rim of the washbasin. The small, dim mirror above the sink reflected pink-lidded eyes and a mouth about to cry. Through her tears, Esther stared at the image in the blotched glass. She seemed to be looking into the eyes of her father.

"Why didn't you call or write?" she whispered. "I had no idea that you were ill. Or that you'd lost the house. After Mother died, you stayed so...remote. You knew how much I wanted to help you."

The bell rang. In five minutes the next class would start. She reached into her purse for her compact and made hasty repairs.

Helen Fitzpatrick joined her at the office mailboxes. "What a nifty suit! Does it come in size 18?" The older woman winked at Esther. "Have you heard the latest? Those bad boys raced through the courtyard again. Nothing on but Mickey Mouse masks. This time they had a girl with them. Minnie Mouse in her bra and scanties."

"Helen, I've just had a conference with Newton. Not good." Esther found a memo in her mailbox. "Now Branscom wants a luncheon chat."

"That means he plans to observe your classes. My advice is to check all the book jackets. The kids like to make 'em—and lose 'em. When Branscom snoopervised my classes, he took note of every book without a cover. I'll never live it down. I know Tom's textbook budget by heart."

"Will I ever get used to this place? At the college, we were told to publish. Here we're pressured to cover the textbooks." Suddenly Esther felt homesick for her former colleagues. She'd enjoyed working with them—and occasionally socializing—but had never found an intimate

friend. During the past five months, she'd lost touch with all of them.

Helen made a gesture as if tipping her hat to Esther. "Want another bit of advice? Gargle with hot salt water. It's the best cure I've found for laryngitis." The starting bell rang as they entered adjoining classrooms.

In her morning classes, Esther gave vocabulary and grammar tests. The first two afternoon classes were almost as quiet. Pupils revised the themes she had corrected. Anyone who did not finish the job in class would have homework. There were few requests for advice or ink for fountain pens, so Esther had time to grade the morning's tests. And remember her brief meeting with Tom Branscom.

This week Branscom was busy with the basketball team. Early next week he'd observe her afternoon classes. "You can count on it!" he'd said as he sprinted away, presumably to the basketball court. She'd never found the chance to mention Augie Dugan. Eighteen, failing English again. And an intimidating student.

As the passing bell rang, she wondered if she felt well enough to deal with Augie and the other members of Period Six. That class always required her to do some talking. She hurried to the lavatory and gargled with hot, salted water.

Everything would be easier if only she had a teaching station of her own. Without one, she had to travel to five different rooms that were available

during her colleagues' free periods. Period Six met in a huge area that belonged to the Home Arts Department. Instead of desks, the room had tables and chairs. Stoves, work counters, and sinks lined the walls. Between tall windows stood a padlocked refrigerator. The large cage on top of it held a motor that never stopped humming. Even on her best days, Esther found the room unsuited to lecturing. Today she'd assign the new books and make sure they got covered.

As she approached the room, she heard Joel Wagner's nasal voice. "Here comes Lovelady!" It was not the first time she'd heard the name. No doubt derogatory, certainly sexual in connotation, it conveyed a meaning to the students that was not at all clear to her.

Water was seeping into the hall. "Please," she whispered, "not today." It had been several weeks since she'd had to pull off her shoes and wade into the classroom.

Augie, a heavyset redhead, lay sprawled across the top of her desk. He seemed to be leering at her. His pale blue eyes looked from her wet stockings up her body to her face. Before she reached the desk, he'd moved to the nearest table.

Esther felt her cheeks getting warm. She looked around for her usual messenger. "Yung Chin, please inform somebody in the front office." The short boy wearing a dark suit and tie began to unlace his shoes and roll up his trousers.

"Budd and Nathan," Esther called, "please turn off the water." With a grand disregard for shoes, kneesocks, and knickers, they raced through the water and closed the taps. Esther sent two girls to get the buckets and mops.

At least no one had started fires in the trashcans this time. She counted seventeen in skirts and twenty-two in long pants, knickers, or stovepipes. All present and accounted for.

Yung Chin returned with the assistant principal. Vincent DeMarco glared at the class. "Who did it?" he demanded. "Dugan, who flooded this floor?"

Augie's face revealed nothing other than the need for a shave. "Beats me," he said. "Honest, Mr. DeMarco, I don't know nothin' about it."

The young administrator borrowed Esther's roll book. He called each name and asked the same question. From Helmut Auerbach through Rosemarie Zupnik, nobody confessed or identified the wrongdoers.

DeMarco organized a relay race to mop up the floor. Satisfied with the results, he made sure that the pupils sat in their alphabetically assigned chairs. Esther had just put on her shoes when he stopped by her desk.

"Miss Lovell, they're all yours now." His tone became confidential. "I'm going to monitor this area. Troublemakers always try again. It's my guess that Dugan is the ringleader."

KALORAMA

"I'm sure you're right. Thanks, Mr. DeMarco."

Esther glanced at the wall clock. Period Six would end in about thirty-five minutes. Quickly she distributed the new books and assigned the first story. She returned to each of the seven tables and handed out book cards and pre-cut paper and tape. "Sign your card, and cover your book. After that, you can read the story. Make sure to finish it before class tomorrow." Each time she spoke, her voice remained clear and steady. The saltwater gargle had helped.

A hand went up, and Esther hurried to see what Felicia Diliberto might need. The buxom, darkly pretty girl smiled at her. "Okay to put my name on the cover?" Stale perspiration, tobacco, Tangee lipstick, and other odors emanated from Felicia.

Esther cupped her hands around her mouth. "Pay attention!" Her resonant contralto voice could be heard above the noise. "Felicia has made a good suggestion. You may put your name and the book title on the cover."

While Esther collected book cards, she checked each cover. Augie had neatly printed his name and the book title. He'd also sketched Mickey and Minnie Mouse, dressed and undressed. The undressed version showed their nude backsides.

No time to make another cover today. There was barely time enough for a few announcements. "You will enjoy these short stories," she said. "The first one is very funny. All of them are about teenagers."

KALORAMA

Several students were talking, and Augie was laughing as he showed his book cover to Felicia. With her heaviest ruler, Esther whacked the edge of the desk. "You are using a new, expensive book," she declared. She looked around to make sure that every pupil was listening. "You must keep it covered at all times. Do you understand me? No uncovered *Teenage Tales!*"

Her last words resounded in the quiet room. The bell rang, but no one moved. Then Augie gave a whoop of pure glee. From every side came whistles and laughter.

What on earth did I say? Esther asked herself. When she caught the pun, the trills of her laughter, melodious and sweet, rippled above the clamor.

Everybody stared at her.

"I outdid myself, didn't I?" she said with a smile.

Augie stood up and tightened the strap around his books. "Yeah, Miss Lovell, it ain't gonna be easy to top that one."

"All of us have better things to do than that," Esther replied. "I'm for making a fresh start. How about you, Augie?"

He looked nonplussed. At the sight of Augie Dugan being caught off-guard, Esther could not keep from laughing. As she glanced around the room, she realized that almost all the other students were laughing with her.

Running, pushing, and shouting, they exploded into the hall. Esther watched them go. Then she

straightened the tables and chairs and collected her things. She'd promised to make a fresh start. The humorous stories were the ideal way to launch it. After that? Drama! *Sunday Costs Five Pesos* was a very funny play. Perfect for a class with so many Spanish-speaking members. Felicia would be marvelous in the fight scene! All the way home, Esther made tentative plans for assigning the other parts.

FEBRUARY

4

Mid went into the pantry expecting to see her husband. He'd gone to pick up the meat, and whenever Nels brought supplies, he always drove the car to the pantry door. Instead, Mid saw the girls.

"What's going on?" she asked. Then she saw Pixie. The little dog was licking a spot on the floor.

"Momma, we had to help her. She was hungry."

"Pixie was crying!" Flo's blue eyes looked shiny.

"What did you give her, Nora?" Mid reached under the sink for the scrub rag to clean the greasy spot on the wooden floor.

"Some kind of meat in the yellow bowl."

KALORAMA

In the icebox Mid saw a shallow depression in the bowl of ground ham. She was scolding Nora when the pantry door opened, and Nels set two bags on the table. "There's more in the car," he said and smiled as the children ran to get it.

Mid watched as he stroked Pixie's ears and black and tan fur. "She's been eating our ham," she said.

"Well, I hope she enjoyed it. Poor little beggar."

Nora added a bag to the others on the table. "Where's Daddy Bill?" She and Flo sat on the floor beside Pixie.

"He stayed to help Eddie. The meat market was busy, and Eddie's helper never showed up."

Mid checked each package before storing it in the icebox. "How did Eddie seem to you?"

"Thin as a rail, but cheerful as ever. He gets such a kick out of swapping yarns with your dad. They were remembering the way kids used to raise hell on the Fourth of July."

"Why has Eddie lost so much weight?"

"I don't know. Bill doesn't either. Eddie's not worried about it, or he'd have seen a doctor."

"Nels, you know what he thinks of doctors. If Eddie's consulted anyone, it's somebody in his church."

"Maybe Bill ought to find out."

"I doubt if he will. He's never understood why Eddie joined that church." She put the last package away. "Nora, it's time to take Pixie

home. You're not to feed her again. Do you hear me?"

"Momma, she was so hungry!"

"Pixie belongs to Mr. Ayres. I'm not at all sure that he wants her to eat ham." Mid gave her husband a sharp look. With a dramatic gesture, he wiped away his offending grin.

"Let's go, kids!" he said. "While you take Pixie home, I'll warm up the engine. You can ride along to the drug store. I might even treat you to single-dip cones! What do you say?"

The girls and Pixie ran to the hedgerow that separated Kalorama from the Ayres' back yard.

"You spoil the child," Mid said. "Why reward her for doing something she knows is wrong?"

"The kids were only thinking of the dog. Anyhow, it's done. I need cigarettes. What can I get for you?"

"Not a thing. I hope Pop comes in time to make the stuffed peppers. We're having two kinds, ham and lamb. Nobody seasons them like he does."

Nels smacked his lips. "Delicious!" he said. "What's for dessert?"

"Pineapple upside-down cake. Whipped cream on the side."

By six o'clock, Nora and Flo had eaten dinner in the kitchen and were heading upstairs. They

walked single file and close to the wall because quite a few boarders were hurrying down to the dining hall. Near the end of the line was a tall man with smiling gray eyes.

"Fancy meeting you here, Nora," Walter Buchanan said. He handed her a manila envelope as he went by her on the stairs.

"Thank you, Mr. Walt!"

"What did he give you?" Flo asked.

"Paper dolls. He used to give them to his little girl. But she's too big now. Come on, let's run!"

They ran to Nora's room. Nora put on the wall lights and dumped the contents of the envelope on the floor. Cardboard ladies lay scattered on the carpet. All of them were beautiful, and all wore fancy underwear or night clothes.

"I love the one with long black hair. She's my favorite." Flo picked up the doll and gave her a kiss.

"That teddy she's wearing is powder blue. Mr. Walt told me that's the latest shade."

"Where does he get the lady dolls? Mine are all little girls."

Nora nodded. "You can't buy these. Mr. Walt cuts them off his boxes. He sells ladies' undies to the stores."

They lined the dolls across the carpet and looked at them.

"Thirty-six," Nora said.

"You're lucky, Nora!"

"Let's leave 'em here. Come with me, Flo." Nora led the way to the butler's pantry that served as the Weigmanns' bathroom.

The long, narrow room lay between her bedroom and her parents' bed-sitting room. From ceiling to floor were walnut doors and drawers. Two white porcelain sinks flanked a large closet. Its door was open and revealed a toilet. In front of the tall window stood a white porcelain bathtub on claw feet.

"Daddy Bill got that big tub at an auction," Nora said. She opened one of the drawers and took out a pasteboard box filled with paper dolls. "Flo, you can pick out thirty-six dolls." She set the box on the hardwood floor.

"To play with right now?"

"For keeps! I had more, but Momma wouldn't let me play with them."

"Why not?" Flo was choosing all the dolls with dark hair.

"Their belly buttons showed. Daddy kept those."

"What for?"

"So Mamma wouldn't give them back to Mr. Walt. That's what she said she'd do. And besides, when Daddy and I play paper dolls, he needs his own to play with. Some day he'll let you see them. Daddy makes gorgeous clothes for his dolls. I can't draw that well — not yet."

Flo was sitting cross-legged on the floor. She seemed to be staring down at her stack of paper dolls. But when she looked up, her eyes brimmed with tears.

"Florence! What's wrong?"

"I want my daddy," Flo said. She hid her face behind her hands.

Nora listened to the sobs. After a while, she got up and went into her bedroom. When she came back, she put the doll with long, black hair on top of Flo's stack.

5

"Mr. Buchanan! Telephone!" Corinna rapped on the door to his room—front and center on Third Floor. The sounds traveled down the quiet hall. It was a few minutes before seven in the morning.

"Be right there!" he called back. Walter Buchanan picked up his overcoat, fedora, and sample case and went down to the first floor. Under the stairs in the entrance hall was a room that housed the telephone as well as umbrellas and coats.

As he had guessed, the call was from Vera, his ex-wife.

"Walt, your darling daughter's done it again. She's really done it this time!" As usual, Vera was shouting into the mouthpiece. He laid the

receiver on the table. Even so, her voice was too loud. He closed the door to the hall.

"Is Skee all right? What happened?"

He could hear Vera striking a match and taking the first long drag on a cigarette. "It all started about four-thirty this morning," she said. "Mom took the call. She never gets enough rest. Not one decent night's sleep since she moved in. She don't look good at all."

"What about Skee?"

"Keep your pants on, Walt! I'm trying to tell you. It was a cop on the phone. He asked was this Stephanie Buchanan's home. Mom told him she was asleep upstairs. But when I checked, no Skee! So I got on the phone. Skee got picked up by the police. Drunk driving."

Walt was getting a familiar queasy feeling. "Skee knows how to drive? Whose car was it?"

"Vinny Cogliano's. He'd passed out in the back seat."

"Cogliano? Is she still running around with that crowd? I thought I'd put a stop to that."

"Hold it a minute, Walt. Mom needs me."

Walt sat back in the armchair. Another mess, but Skee wasn't hurt. Thank God for that. With a sigh, he looked out the window. Nels Weigmann was sweeping the parking area in front of the carriage house. Despite his game leg, he was doing a bang-up job.

KALORAMA

Walt looked around the ten foot room. Brass hooks circled the dark paneled walls. Across from the window and armchair stood a handsomely carved umbrella stand with a beveled mirror, drawers, and shelves. Walt tried to avoid looking at his reflection. He'd already noted the sad face of the tall guy in the gray tweed suit.

Vera was back. "Mom's sick. After I talk to you, I'm calling the doctor."

"I hope she'll feel better soon. Now what about Skee?"

"She's at the Thirteenth Precinct Station. They're holding her for drunk driving and operating a car without a license. And some other things." She left the phone.

"Other things? What other things?" He could hear a cup hitting a saucer and the striking of another match. Damned if he didn't feel like hanging up the phone. Let 'em stew in their own juice for once!

She was back and talking fast. "Skee made trouble when the cops pulled her over. She mouthed off and did some punching. The cop you gotta see is named Daley."

"I'm to see him? Are you telling me to get Skee out of jail? All I have to do is support the two of you." He was glad to hear an edge to his voice.

There was a pause. "Walt, do you think I like asking for this favor? The thing is, my friend Otts

took my car. He's relining the brakes. Besides, Mom needs me."

"Okay, I'll go for Skee." Without waiting for her thanks, he placed a call to the office. The girl on the switchboard had to change his morning appointments.

It began to sprinkle just as Walt turned into Columbia Road. Waiting for pedestrians to cross, he saw Esther Lovell hurrying toward the streetcar platform. What rotten luck! He'd been hoping for the chance to give her a lift. Today's route took him in the opposite direction. He kept glancing at his rear view mirror. Finally he lost sight of her Scottish plaid umbrella. Miss Lovell fit his notion of a real lady.

Showers turned to rain; the rush hour traffic slowed to a crawl. Walt drove almost automatically. Skee had been a pretty child. And smart as a whip! He'd been so proud of Skee, his live doll. Almost as soon as she could talk, she'd given herself a nickname.

Until she started school, he'd often surprised her with playthings he'd made or bought at the dime store. Of course, that kind of fun had ended long ago. Now Skee was seventeen. And in jail! Good God, why had everything gone haywire?

KALORAMA

The traffic lights along Wisconsin Avenue were malfunctioning. As Walt kept pace with other vehicles, he thought about Vera. And their marriage of twenty-five years. Almost from the start, she'd been after him to earn more money. Barely twenty years old, he'd found extra work, and just before their first anniversary, they'd left her mother's flat and moved into rooms of their own. Five years later, they'd made the downpayment on a row house at Thirty-fifth and S Street.

After Skee was born, he'd given her just about all of his free time. While he was in charge at home, Vera shopped. When she wasn't buying clothing for their growing child, she was fixing up some part of the six-room house. Soon he was searching for ways to earn more money. By the time Skee entered high school, he was working sixty hours most weeks—and glad to do it. Over the years he'd come to prefer the orderly routines on the job to the constant bickering at home. Not the kind of life he'd once hoped for—but he'd promised himself to stick with it until Skee got through school. He'd had no premonitions of any major change.

His life with Vera had ended suddenly on a day in November, fifteen months ago. Except for being unusually warm for autumn, that day had begun like many others. Between sips of coffee and bites of toast, Vera talked over the telephone to her mother.

KALORAMA

"Didn't you hear me, Mom? Skee's been expelled! She's already on the train. They caught her with a boy in her room. Yeah, booze, too—the same damn story. Walt's threatening to turn her over to the courts. You know, admit that we can't control our kid. Take it easy, Mom. Walt's mad, but he'd never really do it.

"The point is, Skee's getting here around eleven. Francie's bringing her. Can you beat that? Skee called a friend before she called us. Can you come over and unlock for her? I got this dental appointment. The damn tooth's killing me. No, Skee can't get in. Walt took her key. You know, after that Cogliano mess. You don't remember that one? Walt found the guy in Skee's bed. That was one helluva night! How could anyone forget it? Sure, I understand. Thanks, Mom."

Vera refilled their cups and lit a cigarette. Walt had been expecting to hear what her mother thought of it all. But Vera was scanning the ads in the *Morning Star*.

"What did she say? How much did this fiasco cost her?" Walt hit the dinette table with his fist. "Didn't I warn the pair of you? Sending Skee to that fancy school—another damn fool extravagance! All three of you ought to have your heads examined."

"Mom didn't mention the tuition. But I guess it's gone. Ye gods, the kid didn't last three months! Mom's just worried about Skee. She kept saying,

'Bless her baby heart. Bless her poor little baby heart.'"

Walt took out a folded handkerchief and blotted the dampness on his forehead. "God knows how long it took her to earn that money—standing over that stinking laundry press. She never got one cent the easy way."

"Look, I can't be late to the dentist. We're going to have to iron this out another time."

"Okay, Vera, but I'm telling you right now. Unless I'm in charge around here, things are going to get worse."

"Is that so! We'll just have to see about that." She looked him over. "Say, you got on your new sharkskin suit. Tall guys look swell in double-breasted. I remember now—today's your big day. Well, good luck, fella! Get that palooka on the dotted line!"

"If I land this account, I'll be on the gravy train at last. How's that for an oldtimer?"

"Say, what d'ya mean 'old'? Forty-three ain't old." She gave him a stale tobacco and coffee peck, then headed upstairs.

Walt no longer enjoyed watching his wife climb stairs. Sexy curves had become angles. But he could remember when every male at Central High had kept at least one eye on Vera. Even with both eyes locked in her direction, he'd found it hard to keep in step, and he'd been more surprised than anyone when he actually caught her. The day he'd

KALORAMA

graduated from Central was the day she agreed to be his. That weekend they'd eloped and spent their first night together in the hotel in Elkton, Maryland. In no time at all, Vera got preoccupied with married life—too busy to finish high school.

The rain stopped. Waiting to make a left turn, Walt snapped on the radio and searched for good dance music. How he used to love to dance! He'd been good at it, too—even Vera thought so. "What you need is a big, roomy Dodge with an all-steel body and hydraulic brakes at $645 f.o.b.!" He turned off the radio.

On their wedding day Vera had been all smiles, curves, and upswept blonde hair. She'd enjoyed showing off her heavy gold wedding band, the one his mother had worn all her life. Soon Vera was also displaying a brand new engagement ring—a small but perfect diamond set in a gold love knot. For over a year he'd made time payments. And sacrifices. Hardest by far was giving up tobacco and his prized collection of pipes.

He'd been married for close to ten years before he landed the job he really wanted. As the lingerie representative of Frazier Fashions, he could earn good money—commissions and bonuses as well as a salary. Before Frazier, he'd juggled all kinds of work as well as his classes at the university. A free day had seemed like a vacation to him. One evening he'd said as much to Vera. To his surprise, she'd burst into tears.

"What vacation? All I've done this summer is cook, clean, and take care of Skee." She'd screamed the rest. "I wish I'd never married you! I only did it because I hated school. And I was so tired of worrying that some damn boy would get me in trouble."

Night after sleepless night, he'd lain beside Vera and, without moving or talking, tried to pull himself together. He'd known that she didn't love him the way he loved her, but he'd nurtured the hope that someday she would. That hope was gone. The joy of loving his wife went away.

Near the end of a line of lighted vehicles, Walt waited for his chance to go through the intersection. Odd bits and pieces of his last day with Vera passed through his mind. By noon that day everybody was complaining about the heat. He'd gone home to change into a fresh shirt and grab a bite of lunch. Nothing in the icebox looked easy to fix, so he'd decided to wait. After closing the big deal, he'd celebrate with a poor-boy sandwich and a few beers.

Heading for the stairs, he'd passed the dinette where Vera was sitting. On the table were her Luckies, a coke, and a bottle of aspirin.

He touched her shoulder. "Bad time with the dentist? Your jaw looks swollen."

She shrugged his hand away. "I'm sore as hell at Skee. Home less than an hour, and we've already had a fight."

Walt got some bicarb' and water, then joined her at the table. "Want to talk about it?"

"Gone for months, but she didn't even give her grandmom a hug. Mom had come over to let her in. She'd been waiting here for over an hour. Skee just dropped her bags, borrowed some money, and took off with Francie. Mom said they weren't in the house five minutes. Can you beat that?"

"Have you talked to Skee yourself?"

"Sure, I called over to Francie's. I told Skee to be here for pot roast at 6:30 sharp. And I told her to bring plenty of hugs for her grandmom. The kid wouldn't even promise to come. I got so damn mad I hung up on her." She dropped her cigarette butt in the coke bottle and reached for the telephone.

Walt went to change his shirt. By the time he got back, she was talking on the phone to her mother. "Wish me luck?" he whispered.

"Knock 'em dead, Big Shot!" Because of the novocaine, her smile was more like a grimace.

It had been close to dinnertime when he returned home. Vera and her mother were working in the kitchen. A big feed. Could he get it down? The beers had done nothing for him except to fill him up.

When the telephone rang, he lifted the receiver. Before he said hello, Skee had announced that she would not be home for dinner.

"Your mother told you to be here at 6:30. I'm telling you to hightail it home right now! What?

No, I did not make the deal. This big fish just nibbled. Of course not! Why would I take it out on you? Skee?"

"What was that all about?" Vera had been listening.

"Just doing your job, dammit."

"How late will she be?"

"Your guess is as good as mine." Suddenly Walt felt exhausted. The client had been about to sign—until his partner showed up. "I tried, didn't I?"

"You shot off your big mouth! Mom and I got that part loud and clear."

"What do you mean by that crack?"

"I mean that you're in a lousy mood. You muffed the deal, and you took it out on Skee. Now I've fixed this fancy meal for nothing!" Her face looked flushed and swollen.

Walt knew that his mother-in-law was listening. He'd seen her open the kitchen door. "You and Mom are going to have to face facts. Skee's way out of line. Fancy dinners won't straighten her out. It may take a much firmer hand than mine to do that."

"Up on that same old soap box, Walt?"

He headed for the stairs. He wanted to take off the new suit. The damn trousers didn't fit right.

Vera called after him. "Soup's on in ten minutes! I'll need you to carve the roast."

He didn't like to remember that meal—or what had followed it. At one o'clock in the morning, they'd still been waiting for Skee. He'd got up from his easy chair and snapped off the radio. "You weren't listening, were you, Vera?"

"No, not really. Look at Mom. Out cold. Mom's too old for this kinda stuff."

Vera lay across one-half of the slipcovered couch. Her mother had fallen asleep on the other half. As Walt bent over the sleeping woman, he noticed that beneath a henna rinse her hair was white.

"Poor old girl. Nobody can accuse her of not caring. She started to save that money on the day Skee was born. Good grief, see what she got for it!"

"Mom don't complain. Skee's her only grandbaby. Her big dream! But there's no telling when the kid'll show up. You ought to drive Mom home."

Walt took his mother-in-law's hand. "Wake up, Mom. The party's over. It's time to go home."

She awoke with a start. "I musta dozed!" She tugged at her clothing. "Gee, I wish you'd got me up. I wanted to see her. Bless her baby heart. I hope she don't get sick over all this mess."

Walt helped her to her feet. "Skee never came home. Maybe she's sleeping over at Francie's. Anyhow, it's time for us to get some rest."

KALORAMA

They heard the squeal of tires and the banging of a car door. A moment later, Skee ran into the living room. She was barefoot, and every curve of her slim body showed beneath her red sweater and skirt.

"Where have you been?" Walt bellowed. "Have you any idea of the time?"

"Give the kid a break, Walt." Vera kissed her daughter and picked up her discarded shoes and coat. "Where were you, hon'? We musta made twenty calls."

Skee was searching for something in her pocketbook. She dumped its contents on a chair and poked through the pile, then lit the bent cigarette she'd found.

"Oh, lots of places. A bunch of us ended up in the park at Dupont Circle. David Becker stopped by. Davey's a swell egg! He invited some of us to a party at his flat. His mom's boyfriend lives in Baltimore. She'll be gone all weekend."

Skee pawed through the clutter on the chair and found a small silver flask. She turned unsteadily to show it to them. "See what Vinny gave me?"

Walt stared at her beaded mascara and circles of rouge. He struck the flask from her hand. They both watched as its contents began to seep into the carpet.

"What d'ya go and do that for?" Skee snatched up the flask. "Davey charged me two bucks for this hooch!"

KALORAMA

When she lifted the flask to her mouth, Walt slapped the left side of her face.

She tried again. This time his hand landed hard on her chin. She staggered and fell to her knees.

"My God, Walt, have you gone crazy?" Vera plowed into his chest with her fists. "You keep those big, ugly mitts off my kid!" With all her strength, she shoved him. "Get the hell out of here!"

He stood motionless, as though expecting somebody to stop what was happening.

"Yeah, you heard me, Walt. Get out and stay out! I don't want you anymore."

An impatient driver blew his horn. Walt turned into the parking lot. Glancing at his wristwatch, he saw that it had taken almost an hour to get to the police station. In the rear view mirror, he noticed that he was smiling. And knew why. For fifteen months, he'd been blaming himself for the breakup of his family. Now he understood Vera's part in it. How long had she been waiting for grounds for divorce? Her lawyer had filed suit the following morning.

What a fool he'd been! He'd offered to do whatever they wanted, anything he could do to keep the family together. Finally Vera wouldn't talk to him anymore. Had she been dating another man even then?

A small coupe with a rumble seat pulled out. Walt eased his Olds into the tight space, but

hesitated to turn off the ignition. "Vera's playing me for a sucker again," he decided. "This is her mess. Let her clean it up. I'm getting the hell out of here!"

He hadn't been gone five miles before memories of his little girl began to torment him. One summer—she'd just turned ten—she practically lived in her playhouse. He'd made the house for her birthday, starting with a steam cabinet found at the junkyard. Not an easy remodeling job for him, but the playhouse had made a big hit with her and every other child in the neighborhood.

He remembered another time, several years earlier, when he'd driven nearly twenty miles to get the latest Honey Bunch book. Skee had come down with a bad case of chicken pox. The only thing she wanted was the book, and the only place that had it was out of town. How she'd loved that story! He'd read half of it to her the first night. He could still see the smile on her pox-covered little face.

Sweetest of all were the memories of her at three. She'd watched for him every evening. The moment his car turned into the driveway, she'd come running down the cement path to meet him. "Dee-da, Dee-da!" she called. She couldn't wait to be with him. He'd run, too, to catch her and hold her in his arms. He always got there in time—before she fell and hurt herself.

"We've made a mess of you, baby Skee," he whispered. "All of us have—the family, that rot-

ten crowd you run with, and you. What a goddamn crying shame!"

When the light changed, Walt made a careful U-turn and headed back to the police station. With a little luck, he'd get her home before noon.

6

Nora and Flo were working on their valentines. Lace paper doilies, satin ribbon, crayons, and construction paper covered the kitchen table. Every once in a while, Bill brought them each a cookie. The room smelled of vanilla extract, butter cookies, and cream puffs.

Nora watched as Flo printed X and O on another heart. Dark blue letters looked nice against a red background. "How many, Flo?"

"Forty. I need one more. Forty-two kids in my room."

"Mine, too. One for Miss Deming?"

"I guess so. But no hug and kiss. What did you make for Daddy Bill and your parents?" Nora had been looking at Flo's new dress. The color of the crepe de chine almost matched the blue of her eyes. Nora gave the signal for no talking and passed

three valentines across the table. She whispered, "I'm going to use white ribbon to tie each one."

Except for the name on the top heart, the valentines looked alike. The bottom heart read, "Roses are red/Violets are blue/Sugar is sweet/So are you." Under the hearts was a square of doily.

"They're swell! Mama, Daddy, and Nanna will get cards like these—'cept not so many words. I can't print as good as you. Not yet."

"Will you put X and O?"

"X and O and I love you."

Nora smiled. "I'm going to say that on the backs of mine." She quickly covered the valentines with scraps of doily. Her mother was bringing paper bags to the table.

"Sorry, girls, but Daddy Bill needs to work here. Put your things in these bags. You can work in Nora's room." She distributed the bags and began to clear the table.

"Momma, let us do it! You'll spoil the surprise."

Mid picked some ravelings of ribbon and paper from Nora's rompers. "Okay, but hurry. Daddy Bill can't wait for you."

The girls carried their bags up the stairs. In the hall outside the butler's pantry, Corinna was scrubbing the interior of the dumbwaiter.

"What's that awful smell, Corinna?" Flo asked.

Corinna backed out of the dumbwaiter. "Lysol. Powerful, ain't it? Everything gots to be real clean for tonight."

"What's tonight?" Flo asked.

"Bridge night. Folks plays cards in the drawin' room. Good eats come up from the kitchen on the dumbwaiter. Cold things, then hot. Nora's momma always fix a fancy spread for bridge night."

"How come I never see it?" Flo looked at Nora.

"Where will you be tonight? Where do you go every weekend?"

"Uncle Earl's."

Nora saw Flo's mother coming down the stairs. "I 'spect that's why she has your coat." Lois Haskell handed several garments to her daughter. "Button up, Flo. It's chilly outside." She began to snap a set of furs around her own slender shoulders.

Nora watched as the jaws of one bright-eyed, dark brown animal bit the tail of another. "I'll keep the valentines in my room," she told Flo.

"Mama, do we have to go?" Flo asked.

As if in reply, a tall, stout gentleman in a vicuna topcoat stepped into the hall. "Lois, I call this perfect timing," he said. Earl Shepard tipped his pearl gray fedora and escorted his family out the door.

"They's class!" Corinna said. "Did you see the senator's stickpin?"

"It has a ruby in it."

"Diamonds, too. Ain't none of 'em chips neither." Corinna put the cap back on a can of furniture polish. "This dumbwaiter gots to stay open for a while. Don't you be messin' with it, Nora."

KALORAMA

Nora opened her bedroom door. "I need to finish my valentines."

She set to work, but without Flo it wasn't as much fun to cut hearts and print words. The cards for the kids at school were alike—except for the last one. Roy Williams' card was the only one that said, "Be my valentine." Her initials were on the others. On his, too? She couldn't decide. She slipped his card into her patch pocket.

In the hall she noticed that the doors of the dumbwaiter were closed. The hall was very quiet.

It was quiet downstairs, too. Daddy Bill sat at the kitchen table, which was covered with racks of cream puffs. He cut a generous slit along the side of a bite-sized puff.

"Where are Momma and Daddy?"

"Quick trip to the Seventh Street Wharves. Mid decided that she had to fill half of these puffs with crab salad. Chicken salad's not fancy enough." He gave a snort of disapproval.

"Bridge refreshments?"

"Yep!" Using waxed paper between layers, he stored the puffs in a huge tin canister. "You didn't want one, did you, Nora?"

"Not without custard in it. And frosting on top."

"Me neither." Bill carried the canister to the pantry. When he came back, he selected two perfect hearts from a sheet of cookies and handed them to Nora.

KALORAMA

The cookies soon disappeared. She was asking for more when a door banged, and the sound of angry voices came from the pantry. Nora ran to see what was happening, Bill close behind her.

"Why didn't you say something?" Mid yelled. Her face was flushed. "All that money! I had no idea you wanted dining room furniture." After tossing several packages into the icebox, she slammed it shut.

Nels spoke in almost a whisper. "I do tell you things, but you don't always listen."

"All our savings! An I.O.U. to boot! Have you gone out of your mind?"

"Mid, it was our big chance. Solid walnut, handcarved—china, crystal, linens—everything going for a song. And just right for our dining hall. Even Stanford White would approve!"

"That old lecher's been in his grave for thirty years. You want to please him, but you don't give a hoot about pleasing me!"

Too angry to notice how wet the floor was, Mid stepped into a puddle. The drip pan beneath the icebox had overflowed. She yanked out the pan and started toward the sink, then turned and flung the smelly water at Nels.

Bill grabbed Nora's hand. The sound of shouts and screams followed them to his room behind the dining hall. The noise stopped the moment he shut his door. He led Nora to her favorite chair, a leather lounge beside the rear window.

She sat down, but kept a firm grip on her grandfather's hand. "What's wrong? Why is Momma so cross?"

Bill kissed the top of her head. "Nels went to a hotel auction and bought just about everything in the main dining room. He must have told her about it."

"He told you first?"

"Eddie and I knew about the auction. I talked your daddy into going with us. Nels got a sweet deal. Beginner's luck, I'd say."

"Momma doesn't think so?"

"Nora, your parents love each other, but they don't see eye-to-eye about everything. Not if it means spending a good deal of money."

"Daddy wants furniture. What does Momma want?"

Bill shrugged. "Mid wants to set a fine table." He smiled. "Cream puffs stuffed with crab salad."

He sat down in his easy chair and reached for a copy of *The Nation* on the end table. The magazine had been left open. A full-page cartoon showed Huey P. Long picking his nose.

Nora went to check the bottom shelves of the bookcases. Lined against two of the walls were bookcases, desks, and chairs. On the bottom shelf of one bookcase she found her favorite game, Pollyanna, and the magazines that Daddy Bill got for her at the Next-to-New. On top of an unfamiliar copy of *Child's Life* was a stick of Black Jack gum.

KALORAMA

"Thanks, Daddy Bill. Want half?"

Bill shook his head. He did not look up from the article about Huey. Settled again in the leather chair, Nora looked for an illustrated story. She enjoyed reading in Daddy Bill's quiet room. The only sound was the gentle ticking of his clock. Shaped like a banjo, the clock hung on the wall facing a Murphy bed. Except at night, Bill's bed stood upright behind closed doors.

The clock had just chimed five times when someone tapped, then opened the door, "Oh, sorry! I'm butting in, aren't I?" Douglas Menafee took off his pince-nez and rubbed the red marks on the bridge of his nose.

"Not at all, Doug!" Bill went to shake hands with him. About a month ago, the Menafees had moved into the vacant suite on the second floor.

Nora waited to see where Mr. Menafee would sit. The room had no sofa, but all kinds of chairs. The tall, somewhat stooped gentleman chose the upholstered rocker.

Nora moved to the small writing desk at the opposite end of the room. In its drawer were all sorts of things that could be made into clothes for her paper dolls. Sometimes she'd find a treat of Wilbur buds.

Bill studied the face of his new friend, a former Baltimorean like himself. "What's up? Something amiss in your suite?"

Menafee uttered a sound that was part grunt, part laugh. "At last count, there were five Mmes. in our suite. The old hens are fighting over Anna's party frocks. I couldn't stand it. I took a long walk, but they're still up there."

"Your wife's selling some clothes?" Plump and vivacious, Anna Menafee reminded Bill of his own wife. Had she lived, Elle would be about the same age, he thought.

"One ad in the *Star*, and our sitting room turns into Hutzlers on dollar day." Menafee ran his fingers through his thin, gray hair.

Bill reached into the drawer of an end table and took out a bottle. "Seagram's. Not bad for two bucks a pint. What d'ya say?"

"Why not? Thanks, Bill."

Bill filled two small glasses and put the bottle on a table near his guest.

Menafee took several sips. He rested his head against the overstuffed upholstery of the rocker. "Some of Anna's ball gowns are new. Not likely she'll need formals anytime soon. Believe it or not, she's never blamed me. Not even when I lost the house. She blames Hoover." Menafee reached for the bottle of liquor. "We've lived in Baltimore all our lives. Twenty years in Roland Park. My God, how she misses it! When she thinks I'm sleeping, she cries. And before daybreak I have to get ready to go back to my new job. Back to the Commercial Credit Company and the bottom rung of the corporate ladder."

"Oh? I thought you held an executive position."

"I'm their disbursing auditor. Nobody's hiring executives. Nothing at all for me in Baltimore. I was lucky to find this job, but it keeps me on the road a lot."

"Quite a change. For your wife, too."

"We're getting used to it. Now that we live here, she's not so lonely." Menafee set aside his glass. "My wife's been used to gracious living and lots of company. There was nothing gracious and friendly about the last place we rented. The minute she saw Kalorama, she wanted to move in."

Nora lost interest in what they were saying. She hadn't found candy, but she had found a bunch of used envelopes. All of them had fancy linings, and one of them looked like a sheet of pure gold. She reached into her pocket for Roy's valentine. Add a gold heart? She was tracing and cutting when she realized that Daddy Bill was talking about a murder.

"The judge went along with the insanity plea. Thaw got away with murder."

"Crime of passion? That's what the rags called it. They dished that dirt for months—racy stories about Stanford White and Thaw's wife."

"The girl in the red velvet swing." Bill sighed. "I saw Evelyn Nesbitt in a stage show. I'll never forget her."

"Pretty as her pictures?"

KALORAMA

"The most beautiful woman I've ever seen."

Someone knocked, then opened the door. Mid's eyes were red. She nodded to Menafee and spoke in an undertone to her father. "I'm short-handed, Pop. Nels isn't here. Can you come right away?" After a brief exchange with him, she beckoned Nora.

Nora put the valentine in her pocket and swept everything else into the drawer. Before leaving the room, she blew a kiss to Daddy Bill.

"You'll be having dinner in the dining hall tonight," her mother told her. "I laid out your yellow dress."

Nora was only half-listening. Her mind was on Roy's valentine. One side of the gold heart would ask, Guess Who? On the other side he'd find the answer. In tiny letters.

Mid awoke and reached across the bed for her husband. He wasn't there. She pulled the chain of her bedside lamp and looked at the clock. Way too early to start breakfast. When Nels was gone, she never slept well. Her damned Irish temper had driven him away. He'd stormed out with water dripping from his hat and bits of vegetables clinging to his overcoat.

And he'd missed the bridge party. Nels loved to play cards, especially auction bridge, and he was a

whiz at the game. He'd been Walter Reed's champion player.

Without Nels for his partner, the colonel lost every rubber. And Letty Flagglar missed Nels' jokes. She enjoyed passing them along to her ladyfriends. Even with three tables of players, the drawing room had seemed quiet.

At least the puffs went over big. When Anna Menafee asked for the crab meat recipe, Pop actually told her the secret ingredient. "Capers!" He'd never shared his secrets with his restaurant customers. "I toss in whatever happens to be handy," he'd said. And it was the truth. Most of his discoveries had been made that way.

In the cold bathroom, Mid settled for a quick spongebath. To brighten her navy wool jumper, she chose a long-sleeved jersey blouse, Nels detested its colors—lime green and electric blue. She added a navy cardigan sweater, then went down to the kitchen.

After a brief search for matches, she lit the gas in one oven. It was too early to fire up the furnace. Besides, she reminded herself, shoveling coal was not her job.

The cast iron and white porcelain stove had four ovens and eight burners. She lit the gas under the percolator. Thirty years ago, somebody had chosen this stove for embassy use. Mid ran her fingers around a burner. It was as smooth as gunmetal. Only lye water and elbow grease could keep

a range this clean. "You're an old beauty," Mid whispered. "If I have anything to do with it, you'll stay beautiful."

Nels didn't understand—not really. "Why is Corinna using steel wool on those pans? My God, Mid, they're already like mirrors!" She'd told him, "It's not enough to own nice things. You have to keep them nice." But Nels knew very little about such work—or the joy of it. So she'd put herself in charge of Corinna. No one had complained.

In the warmth coming from the open oven, Mid breakfasted on coffee and leftover puffs. When Nels tastes these, she thought, he'll know why I had to get the crab meat. But whatever possessed him to buy fancy furniture? In times like these, who expects carved walnut? Well, obviously Nels does.

Everything on the first floor of Kalorama had come from the Weigmanns' home in Ann Arbor. An only child, Nels expected to inherit more, but his father had left big debts so a good many nice things had to be sold. His long-time neighbor bought most of them. Even during the funeral she'd pestered Nels about the house itself. "That dumb-Dora's got more dollars than sense!" he'd said. Two months later—was it really that soon?—she'd made a tempting offer, and Nels grabbed it. He'd already seen Kalorama and fallen in love with the place. He still felt that way. Lots of times he'd look around with a lovesick smile on his face.

KALORAMA

Nels had managed to make the down payment on Kalorama and pay for some repairs. But God bless Pop! With his help, they'd completed the remodeling. Leaving the old neighborhood had been hard for Pop—he'd said so more than once—but selling his restaurant had been a cinch. The new owners were already running the business when the stock market began to go crazy. Pop survived the crash. "By the skin of my teeth," he'd said. "I was going to bank the money, but I couldn't decide which one to trust. So I've still got it. Every cent of it! For the time being, we're cash customers."

She set her dishes in the sink and found recorded music on the radio. Mid sang along to the tunes from *Anything Goes* until the dishes were done and the German-silver faucets and white porcelain sink were shiny.

In the pantry she surveyed the shelves. Whoever said she had to buy ice cream every Sunday? For dessert they'd have apricots. I'll stew 'em with plenty of sugar and lemon, she decided. Jelly roll on the side because Nora loved it.

After the fight in the pantry, Nels didn't know where to go. He didn't want to go anywhere. All day he'd been looking forward to the bridge party—his first chance to play against Menafee.

KALORAMA

The guy talked a good game.

When he reached The Oasis, his favorite bar, Nels kept driving. He was not in the mood to tie one on. Without planning it, he found himself heading back to the old neighborhood—to Bill's former restaurant and Southeastern University.

He parked in front of Eddie's Market. The store was closed for the day, but lights shone in the flat above. Eddie Lyons had been working and living here for most of his adult life—ever since his grandfather had died and left it to him.

Eddie showed a lot of white, crooked teeth when he smiled. He brushed something from Nels' sleeve and pumped his hand. "Come on in, kid!" he said. "I hope you brought your appetite along. I just smothered a choice piece of round, and the darn thing's at least a mile long."

He led the way through the small vestibule, up a long flight of stairs and down a hall crowded with bookcases, wall clocks, and a gigantic rosewood secretary-desk. In the living room, he handed Nels the full tumbler that had been waiting on the gate-leg table.

"Bottoms up, kid! I'll join you in two shakes of the lamb's tail."

While Eddie banged around his kitchen, Nels sipped Jack Daniels and studied the living room. It seemed more crowded than the last time he'd seen it. In some ways, it reminded him of Bill's room.

KALORAMA

Each piece seemed distinctive, but nothing matched. Unlike Bill, Eddie did not go in for pictures. A framed NO SMOKING sign was the only wall decoration. Stamps littered the leather top of a mahogany desk. The oak desk, a roll-top, revealed jars of Indian pennies and stacks of silver coins. A gilded curio cabinet held bundles of correspondence and photograph albums, so many that the door had to stand ajar.

Eddie was back and looking, Nels thought, as though he'd just gone over himself with cleanser and a scrub brush. In his butcher shop, Eddie always seemed to be wearing a spotless apron. How did the guy manage to stay so clean?

Eddie filled Nels' nearly empty glass, then his own. "I got the booze from one of my customers. Prince of a guy—been out of work for a devil of a long time. Used to stop by the market just as I was closing. I'd have a bag waiting for him—soup bones and stuff I couldn't sell the next day. Well, I come to find out that's how they scraped by—on whatever I'd dropped in the bag." Eddie took a small sip of whisky, then set his drink aside. "He had his kid with him when he gave me the present. Little redhead—reminded me of Bill when he was seven or eight—when we both lived on Asquith Street. Holy Smoke! Nearly sixty years ago! Back in Baltimore. When I heard they'd been living on my bags, I tell you, Nels, I nearly busted out crying."

Nels looked at the table, at the fried steak and onions, store bread, canned tomatoes and applesauce. "Eddie, this is swell," he said.

"Dig in, kid!"

Nels enjoyed the food. He helped himself to more when Eddie passed him the serving dishes, but hesitated to take the last slice of meat. The platter had never held more than one generous portion. "What about you, Eddie?"

"Eat all you want, Nels. If you don't get it down tonight—Suffering Cats!—I'll have to eat it tomorrow."

Nels noticed that Eddie had eaten very little.

"Coffee, Nels? Glad to make it for you. I got plenty on the shelf."

"No thanks, Eddie. But I could use another shot or two."

"Sure, kid, help yourself!" Eddie moved the bottle across the table, then collected the dirty dishes in one large hand. When Nels tried to help, Eddie waved him aside. "No room for more than one bottle-washer in this greasy spoon."

"Eddie, can you put me up for the night? I'd stretch out on your sofa. All I need is a blanket."

"I can do you one better than that. I got me a rollaway in the bedroom. We'll roll it in here anytime you say." He grinned. "How come I get the honor of your company? Don't you usually bunk with one of your army buddies?"

Nels poured another swallow into his glass. "I guess I'm sort of homesick for the old days. Before Kalorama."

Eddie chose an overstuffed armchair. "Me, too, kid. It sure was swell when Bill lived on the block. Strange how things work out. He and Eleanor moved to Washington before I did. Her folks lived here." Eddie gave a big sigh. "Remember how we used to pick crabs?"

"That's what you were doing the first time I met the two of you—picking steamed crabs and drinking beer."

"Yeah, I remember. Mid had met you over to the university. What was that course you two were taking?"

'Hotel Management. Uncle Sam was paying, so I stuck with it—all the way to diploma. Mid never got hers, though."

With a chuckle Eddie said, "She got you instead! Sure, I remember that day. It was a Monday so the restaurant was closed. Bill and I spent the day in Annapolis. We rented a rowboat and went crabbing. Holy Moses, you never saw so many blue crabs!"

"They were bright red when I saw them. I couldn't decide what was redder—the crabs or Bill. What a sunburn!"

"He kept splashing it with cold tea, remember?"

Nels nodded. "And saying it was nothing compared to when he was a kid."

"Well, he got that right. All summer long Bill went from burn to blister. But what a time we had! We'd spend all day swimming in the harbor. Or riding the trolley to Sparrows Point. Once in a while, we'd take the ferry to Tolchester. If we hung around with the kids on the block, we played stickball. Sometimes the game ended in a rock fight." He reached for his drink. "No sissies on Asquith Street!" He walked across the room to sit in a straight chair.

"When did Bill start to read? I mean, really go in for books?"

"Bill always went in for books. I guess he turned into a first class bookworm when Elle came down with TB. After work, he just went home and stayed there." Eddie took small sips from his glass.

"Why didn't he get it? Or Mid?"

Eddie shrugged. "I don't know. Most families had somebody spitting and dying. Mid was still in diapers when her mother died." He carried his glass to the kitchen, then went into the adjoining bathroom. He stayed so long that Nels wondered what was wrong. Eddie seemed restless, not in the mood to sit around and unload a few problems. Nels felt a bit edgy himself. He needed a smoke.

When Eddie returned to the living room, he looked tired and old. "I'm going to have to call it a day. Want to give me a hand with the cot?"

Nels smiled, but shook his head. "Thanks for the swell chow, Eddie—and the memories. But I've decided to shove off for home."

"You're sure, kid?" Eddie took a deep breath and slowly let it out. He smiled his toothy smile, and shook Nels' hand.

At the end of the block Nels paused long enough to light a cigarette. And to change his mind. Pete Munden's flat was no more than ten minutes away. On Saturday nights Pete always got some buddies together for poker.

Nels glanced at his pocket watch. Going on eight. He checked the contents of his wallet. Not flush, but enough for a few hands—maybe more. For some reason he didn't understand, he suddenly felt lucky.

MARCH

7

"I dare you!" Flo whispered. She tiptoed through the open doorway into Col. Smith's suite.

Nora did not follow her. But she wanted to. It was another rainy afternoon, and she couldn't decide what to play. She watched as Flo walked around the colonel's sitting room. Flo was wearing rompers. Momma had added patch pockets, but the rompers were a pair that Nora had outgrown.

"I double-dare you!" Flo called and began to skip along the hardwood floor that bordered the big blue carpet. She passed windows, bookcases, chairs, the poker table, and gun cabinet. "Come

on, Nora! He's gone to a party. Dinner and cards. I heard him say so."

"Shhhhh! Corinna's in the drawing room."

"Fraidy cat!" Flo jumped onto the brown leather sofa that faced the fireplace and a closed door. She pointed to the door. "What's back there?"

"His bedroom. It was going to be the embassy office, but Kalorama never got to be an embassy. I can tell you about it. I know a whole lot of stories about this house. Let's go to my room and play story time!"

Flo headed for the colonel's bedroom. "Come back!" Nora called. She ran into the sitting room and called again. Flo did not appear or answer, but it was easy to find her. She stood beside the colonel's bed, a massive four-poster. It was hard to see anything clearly because both sets of heavy window drapes were closed. Nora recognized the scent of bay rum.

Flo reached for Nora's hand. "What's back there?" A little light entered from under a door in the rear of the room.

"A hall. It goes to the biggest bathroom in the house. It used to be a tap room, but Daddy changed it."

"Tap room?"

"It's got a counter with a brass rail, lots of shelves, and an icebox. Daddy put most of the tables and chairs in the dining hall. He got a bathtub and wardrobe closets for here."

KALORAMA

They were about to enter the bathroom when strong hands grabbed them.

"What you girls doin'? Snoopin'? Shame on you!" Corinna's face looked chalky in the dim light. She slapped their legs and scolded them all the way back to the front hall.

"Quit worrying, Mid!" Nels said. "Everything's fine and dandy. God knows, Bill's had to cover for me. Now I get the chance to return the favor. I'm glad he decided to stay with Eddie. That poor guy needs help. He couldn't even stow his own gear at the hospital."

"Which hospital?"

"Woodbine. Eddie's church runs the place. Bill argued against it, but Eddie won't go anywhere else. Until this morning, I'd never seen Eddie get really mad."

"What's wrong with him?"

"He claims he's just run down. Bill tells him that he's kidding himself." Nels sighed. Eddie had looked worse than ever. A gray bag of bones. But why upset Mid? She'll find out soon enough. Nels displayed a platter of thinly sliced ham.

"Parsley. And use the can of pineapple in the icebox." She lifted a heavy pot from the oven. The aroma of beans, salt pork, and molasses filled the kitchen.

Nels went into the pantry. "Ready for the molded salads?" he called.

"Just the big one."

"Mrs. Weigmann, I put up the buffet table. You want for me to take in the ham?" Corinna was dressed for dinnertime in her black uniform and starched white apron and cap.

"Take the bean pot and ladle." Mid was unmolding fruited jello, but managed a nod toward the stove. After the maid had left the kitchen, Mid said, "Corinna spanked the girls today."

"Whatever for?"

"She found them in Smitty's bedroom. The girls didn't say a word. She told me about it."

Nels washed his hands and dried them on the roller towel. "The kids deserved to be punished. But spanking them is not her job. I'll make damn sure she understands me."

"That's pretty much what I said to her—and I was nice about it. Nels, go easy on Corinna. We don't want to lose her."

Corinna entered the kitchen and picked up the glass plate holding the molded salad. "I ain't fixin' to go nowheres," she said and headed back to the dining hall.

Nels winked at Mid.

She laughed. "That reminds me. Bobbie told me that she'll be away for a while. Mexico. With her brother."

"For how long?"

KALORAMA

"Why not find out? She always comes early for buffet."

He put on his jacket and adjusted his tie. "I'll greet folks until she shows up. Then I'll get the details. She's been planning this trip for months."

Bobbie McElroy had been at the General Accounting Office when word came that her brother was in surgery. She had telephoned for a taxicab and appointed Janet Wilson to supervise the typing pool. With Janet in charge, the work would get done. Janet was an able, well-mannered young woman. At the moment, she was living in a rooming house unsuited to gentlewomen. The best way to help Janet was to get her out of there and into Kalorama. Nels had promised to let her have the first vacancy on Third Floor.

In less than half an hour, Bobbie was entering the spacious grounds of St. Elizabeth's Asylum. It was a cloudy, windy January morning. Patches of snow clung to the black roofs of the sentry station, chapel, and huge brick buildings. The sentry waved the cab on.

"It's like a college campus," Bobbie said to the driver. "White columns and big porches. Marvelous old trees."

"Mighty pretty place. Why waste it on a bunch of loonies?" Bobbie made no comment. He let her out at the Davis building.

KALORAMA

Avoiding the worst puddles, she hurried toward the entrance. The breeze felt damp as well as cold. She was rubbing her gloved hands and stamping her galoshes by the time the door was unlocked.

"How's my brother?"

"Still in surgery," the receptionist said. "Lester punched out a few windows. That's all I know. Dr. Myers wants to see you, but there'll be a bit of a wait." She unlocked the door to the lounge.

The large, gray green lounge served visitors as well as patients. Bobbie hung her coat and scarf on the rack and chose an armchair beside a front window. She lit a cigarette. Nothing to do but wait. And pray. For more than twenty years—ever since Lester got sick—she'd done a lot of both.

At the far end of the lounge was the door to the ward and a desk where an attendant was assembling papers. From time to time he quieted a patient who sat cross-legged on the floor. Although the room was comfortably warm, the elderly man kept calling for more heat. He was using an army overcoat like a blanket. Near the center of the room, three younger patients shared a sofa. They looked a lot alike—thin, clean-shaven men in faded green sweaters and slacks. They faced a console radio. No one smiled, not even when the radio audience laughed. Bobbie recognized the voices of "Vic and Sade."

Two teenagers entered. Compared with the other patients, they looked well dressed in dark

suits and white shirts. No belts or neckties. One of them began to walk up and down the long room. He walked quickly and with a steady pace. The other boy remained near the door to the ward. He stood unsupported on one leg.

As the minutes passed, Bobbie's concern for him grew. Finally she went to the attendant. "Can't you get this youngster to sit down?"

"It's no use. Ned just stands up again. If his folks don't show up soon, I'll take him back to the ward. The nurse may put him in restraints for a while."

Bobbie positioned her chair for a better outdoor view. On both sides of the street were huge trees, their bare limbs silhouetted against the pale gray sky. Suddenly the man with the overcoat brushed against her chair. He was heading for the water fountain. After a noisy drink, he urinated in the nearby corner where the floor was already damp. As he retraced his steps, he paused beside Bobbie and demanded cigarettes. She looked for the attendant, but he and the boy had left the lounge.

"No cigarettes!" she declared and shook her head. For a few seconds, the old man studied her face. Then he chose a place on the floor where he faced a tall radiator.

Years ago, Bobbie had learned to use gestures and few words when she had to talk with patients. Once in a while she found it hard to communicate with Lester. He'd regard her with suspicion and

refuse to accept her gifts, not even cigarettes, candy, or sodas.

During Sunday's visit, Les had talked nonsense about helping the Kaiser to build asylums. Quite a few patients had seemed disturbed that afternoon. It took three orderlies to haul one large, angry man back to the ward. "I ain't nobody's damn nigger!" he shouted. "Ain't no white trash gonna bad-mouth me!" He spat in the direction of someone he'd wrestled to the floor. That man covered his head with his shapeless green sweater and protected it with his arms. He stayed like that until one of the orderlies came for him.

Now Bobbie heard the sound of a key being turned in the door lock. The receptionist admitted a new visitor, a pretty woman in a well-cut tweed overcoat. The newcomer tried to embrace the boy. He pulled away and continued his pacing. She caught up with him and smiled and talked as if he could understand what she said. Finally she forced him to sit and taste a cookie she'd made for him. Within seconds, he'd given the bag of cookies to the men on the sofa. He went back to pacing. Soon she was trying to match her short strides to his long ones.

Bobbie lit another cigarette. She wanted to look elsewhere, but kept glancing at the walkers. The pretty blond was trying so hard to reassure the boy. Her son? Bobbie sighed. For a very long time, she'd done the same sort of thing. She'd refused to

believe that her brother would always be sick. Nobody knew how to get him well.

Twenty years ago, the doctors hadn't even kept him safe. They'd let him celebrate his twenty-first birthday at the farm. "We're giving Les a weekend pass," they'd told her. "After such a long drive, he'll need a good night's sleep so he's well rested for his big day."

His big day. Awakened by the rooster, she'd hurried into her clothes and gone down to the kitchen, fragrant with fresh baked pies.

"Morning, Gram!" She'd bent to give and receive a kiss.

Gram stood four feet ten. Her starched housedress had her own tatting around the collar and cuffs. She had finger-waved and brushed her thin white hair into a knot on top of her head.

"Bobbie, them pies is done, Four big 'uns. Will you lift 'em out for me?" Gram watched as the pies were stored in the nearby cupboard, then opened the kitchen door and let in some cool air. "Ain't them maples fine? The cold snap done it." She pointed to a sunlit line of red, orange, and gold trees.

"October's been a pretty month in Washington, too."

"What do you think of the birthday pies? Blackberry. And I made apple dumplings."

"Lester's favorites! I bet he'll want dumplings and cream for breakfast."

KALORAMA

"You wake him up now. It's time for breakfast. I want you to take him to Somerset this morning. The county fair's real good this year, but mind you get home by noon. Folks are expecting dinner at one sharp." Gram had almost pushed her through the door and onto the back porch.

Les had insisted on sleeping in the barn—although Gram had given his bedroom a special scrubbing, curtains and all.

"Oh, he can sleep where he wants," Gram had said. "Les always did like being to himself. There's a cot in the loft, and he don't care if them sheets ain't clean."

Years ago, Les had moved some of his belongings to the unused loft in the barn. It was a great place for the old gramophone and records, his drawings of birds and animals, and the Indian artifacts he'd unearthed. On a shelf above the cot was his water collection—Mason jars of water from the Atlantic Ocean, Susquehanna River, Gulf of Mexico, and every other body of water he'd ever seen.

Near the top of the ladder to the loft, she'd had a good view of his boyhood treasures. "Breakfast time!"

Les lay motionless in a tangle of bedclothes. "Apple dumplings and cream!" she'd called in a loud voice. Still no response, so she'd climbed into the loft and tugged at his covers. The quilt felt sticky. There were reddish-brown stains on it. "Oh, Les, what have you done?"

The pistol lay beside him. There was a small hole near his right ear.

Unaware that Dr. Myers had entered the lounge, Bobbie was startled when he spoke to her. "How's my brother?" she asked.

"Lacerations, some of them deep," he said. "We stitched him up, and he'll be okay. Of course, he won't be using his right hand and arm for a while." The doctor's brown eyes looked large behind his gold-rimmed glasses. "Physical therapy may be indicated—but not the ordeal he went through years ago."

"Is he in a lot of pain?"

"He'll be uncomfortable for a while. That won't make life easier for any of us, will it?" He smiled. "Don't worry, Miss McElroy. For everybody's sake, we'll keep Les sedated for a few days." He shook hands with her.

"I'd like to see him."

"Okay, but don't wake him. Sleep's the best medicine." He led her through the ward, beyond the nurses' station, and into a small private room.

Bobbie stared at her brother. His face looked as white as the tightly drawn sheets, as white as the scalp showing beneath his short, dark hair.

"Bobbie?" Lester's voice sounded groggy. "I was…dreaming. Uncle Nevin was showing me…how to stucco. Remember that hotel we built?"

Dr. Myers interrupted him. "Lester, listen to me. The nurse will bring you something to help you

sleep. Until then, your sister can visit. Understand?" He looked at Bobbie. She nodded, and he headed for the door.

"When did I go...to Guadalajara?" Lester asked.

The room had no chair so Bobbie sat at the foot of the bed. "You'd just graduated from Somerset High. Uncle Nevin offered to teach you the construction business." She watched as Lester tried to move his bandaged arm. "A good dream?"

"The best time I ever had. Why does my arm hurt?"

"You punched out some window glass. What made you do that?"

One eyelid drooped, but his eyes looked clear and bright. Blue, deep-set eyes like her own. "They make promises," he whispered. "But they don't always keep them. I get...so damn mad!"

She was finding it easy to understand what he said. He speech was halting—it always was—but he didn't stutter or use strange words.

Lester's chest began to heave. Soon he burst into loud sobs. At the sight of his wet face and twisted mouth, Bobbie's eyes filled with tears.

"I know your arm hurts," she said. "But it's going to get well. The nurse is bringing something to help you."

He shook his head. "It's not my arm. Don't you see? I can't...take it anymore. Why does God leave me here? Will it always be this way? Help me, Sis."

KALORAMA

She took a towel from the washstand and dried his tears. Then she dried her own.

"Yuj lut xybrolad kamiz!" he said.

"What? I don't understand you, Les."

He talked and talked, but she could not make sense of anything he said. He seemed to be angry with someone. Sometimes he got angry with her, too, especially if she couldn't recall the way things were done at the asylum—or other places he had known. Their best times together were when they talked about growing up on the farm.

Les couldn't share everything with her. He'd been a newborn infant when their mother died of childbed fever. Not quite eight years old, Bobbie had packed her own clothes and helped her father pack the baby's things. She did not recall the drive from Pittsburgh to the farm, but she did remember the way Gram had hugged her and cried. Gram was in mourning for her daughter, her only child.

For a long time their father had spent his weekends at the farm. Bobbie had clear memories of him, although he'd stopped coming even before her tenth birthday. Les had no memories of his father—or the young woman who never really acted like their stepmother.

What did she remember? The girl's hat wreathed in veils and flowers, the big coconut cake they'd eaten on the porch, and Gram's first words after they'd left. "It's settled. You're staying here with me. Why, I wouldn't trust them to do a

good job of raising Two Bits!" Two Bits was Gram's Airedale.

So many memories of Gram, Les, and herself. Sis. Ages ago that had been her name.

Several weeks later, Bobbie met with Dr. Myers. They shared a wooden bench in his office, a room full of filing cabinets and stacks of books. He listened to her plan and said nothing at all until she asked for his opinion. Then be answered quickly, confidently, almost as though he'd memorized the words.

"Some day medical science will come to our rescue. I have no doubts about that. Somewhere in this world, cures for mental illness will be found. Soon, God willing. In the meantime, all anyone can do is provide sanctuary and state-of-the-art care." He looked into her eyes. "Forget your plan. It would put Lester at risk and possibly break your kind and generous heart. Lester's very sick. He'd let you down."

"If I don't get him out of here, he'll run away."

"Let him. Lester's not used to bread lines. If he manages to slip out, he'll come back."

"He swears that he'll kill himself instead."

Dr. Myers managed a small smile. "Are our accommodations that bad? Of course not. Lester's bluffing."

KALORAMA

"I wish I could believe you. Most nights—if I manage to sleep at all—I have the same nightmare. I'm running as fast as I can, but my little brother always runs faster. I wake up just as he's jumping off the Calvert Street bridge."

Later that week, Bobbie told Lester that she was planning a vacation for him. Right away he wanted to know more about it. As soon as she told him the gist of her plan, he was eager to go. There was no more talk of suicide. All Les wanted to talk about was his vacation and the arrangements for it. As promised, Bobbie advertised for a companion for Les, received letters, checked references, and held interviews. By the time she'd finished the job, Lester had regained the full use of his arm.

On an afternoon in early March, Bobbie was waiting for the applicant they had chosen. At the sound of the knocker, she opened the front door at Kalorama and stared up at James Hurley. He was blond, sunburned, and smiling. "My word," she exclaimed, "you're so young!"

"I'm twenty-seven. I thought you knew."

She watched a flush spread across his freckled face. She'd been staring. "Relax, Mr. Hurley," she said. "You know the job's yours. I don't know why, but I've pictured you as older and sort of weather-beaten. I wasn't expecting you to be so good looking."

His flush deepened. She smiled and led him into the drawing room. "Put your coat anywhere," she said. "We have this room to ourselves for as long as we need it." She watched as he draped his pea jacket and muffler over the arm of a Hepplewhite chair. "Where would you like to sit?"

He walked to the sofa facing the fireplace. She chose an upholstered armchair nearby and stretched her legs across its ottoman.

"Nice place," he remarked. He seemed to be studying her resoled oxfords.

"When I'm here, I almost forget what's happening everywhere else. Oh, I'm not the owner! This is a boardinghouse."

He glanced at the crystal chandeliers. "I didn't know this kind existed."

"It was a private home until a few years ago. And almost became an embassy—but that deal didn't work out. I should thank hard times for bringing me here."

"That goes for me, too, I guess." He rubbed his large hands back and forth across his knees. "Did you get the tickets?"

"Yes, but I've made a few changes."

His eyes widened. "No Sunday sleeper?"

"Yes, but I'm going along. I've taken a compartment for Lester and me…and a lower berth for you. Les and I will travel the whole way together. You'll buy the automobile and the other things just as planned, then join us at the house in

Guadalajara. The rental sounds good, but I must see it to make sure. After you get there, I'll head for home." She noticed the tightening of his jaw.

"You don't trust me?" he said.

"Yes, I do. Why wouldn't I? All your references checked out just fine. You've been given the seal of approval by Weigmann and Norris. And my brother likes you. Mr. Hurley, if I didn't trust you, you wouldn't be here. The person I can't trust is Lester. You'll be going a long way by car. During that part of the trip, he might disappear. There are things about my brother..."

"Yesterday he wanted to tell me something, but he couldn't control the stutter. Boy, did that frustrate him!"

"When he was twenty-one, Les shot himself. The bullet went through his brain and lodged in his skull. It's still there. For a long time he couldn't talk at all. Or do much of anything. He had to learn the basics all over again. Of course, he'll always be impaired."

"He's deaf in one ear?"

"Yes, and close to blind in one eye. Mr. Hurley, let's get to the point. Lester regards you as his friend. He'd like to spend a year in Mexico with you. But can you put up with him? Schizophrenia is his biggest problem, but it's not his only one. Is there any chance of your backing out?" She watched his face. His expression did not change.

"I want this job, Miss McElroy. You have my word that Lester and I will stick together. He'll be safe with me." He shook his head when she offered him a cigarette. "I'll try to give him a good year. Choices of things we can do. At night—when he doesn't need me—I'll work on my book."

"What book?"

"I grew up on clam boats. I'm from the eastern shore of Virginia. This job will let me write about it. That's the main reason I answered your ad."

She nodded. "Write whenever he doesn't need you. Years ago, Les loved to read. He might enjoy listening to your story." She led the way to a secretary-desk. "My lawyer drew up our agreement. Look it over. My signature is on both copies. We need yours."

He sat at the desk and read the document. Then he went through it again, occasionally pausing to study parts of it.

Why is he taking so long? Bobbie wondered. Is he finding things he didn't expect? She sat on the piano bench and tried not to watch him.

"Your lawyer thought of everything, didn't he? It's all here, and I can't fault any of it." He signed both copies and pocketed one of them. "You even included a bonus."

"The bonus was the lawyer's idea. Whenever the going gets rough, remember the bonus. It will be yours at the end of the year. In fact, if Lester tells me it was a good vacation and still regards

you as his friend, I'll sweeten the pot. That's a promise, Jim."

Sitting on a rattan settee that was screened by potted cactus plants and palms, Bobbie looked around the lobby. Tourists in embroidered cottons and sandals were buying tickets for tours, postcards, and souvenirs. It seemed like years since she'd said goodbye to Nels and Mid. She felt tired and very out of place in her navy traveling suit.

A well-groomed, balding man was approaching her. He took off his spotless panama hat. "Miss McElroy? Clarence Reid. Welcome to Guadalajara!" Without invitation, he positioned himself and his hat on the settee. "How was the trip?"

She groaned. "Exhausting. My brother's on strong sedatives, so he'll sleep all morning. No one warned me. I thought it would be easy to come by train." She tried not to remember the last part of the journey. Without Jim, it had been anything but easy to manage Lester.

Reid looked sympathetic. "Uncomfortable beds? But the Estrellita is one of our best hotels."

"The beds are fine, but a little dog yapped and cried for hours. I'm not sure I'm up to inspecting the house."

His sympathetic expression disappeared. "Ordinarily I don't reserve my rentals. 'First come,

first served,' you know. But you told me that your brother is a convalescent. I've been holding the perfect place for him. Comfort and seclusion. Why not take a quick look?"

Too tired to argue, Bobbie followed him to his car. The black Packard, far from new, gleamed with polish. Its well-upholstered front seat felt comfortable, and beside her window a glass vase held a spray of fresh flowers. Reid handled his motorcar as if he enjoyed driving. Bobbie began to relax.

"Everything looks so pretty," she said. "So many flowering trees! Last night I got a different impression of Guadalajara."

"Poinciana trees. You're seeing the best part of town." He called her attention to water sparkling in an immense marble fountain. "That section near the station—well, you won't have to go there for a while."

She did not bother to correct him. "I'm not used to children begging. One of them looked no older than four or five. She was so dirty and tired but trying to sell a little wooden burro. Lester needed me, or I would have chased after her and bought it."

"The poor are always with us. Isn't that what the Good Book says? My wife and I hail from Wisconsin. We left in '27 when folks were living high on the hog. Everybody thought we were nuts to sell and come here. But look how conditions have changed in the States!"

KALORAMA

He turned into a dead-end street lined with oleanders in full pink bloom. "That last house—behind the palmettos—has everything your brother needs!"

He parked in front of the two-story adobe house. Bougainvillea covered most of its facade.

"The vine's gorgeous, but it needs pruning," Bobbie said. "Lester needs leg room. This house looks small."

"It's bigger than it looks. None of the older homes have much frontage. Four good-sized rooms surround the patio, a nice one. Two rooms upstairs—smallish but they share a balcony overlooking trees. And a thicket. You might say Mother Nature did the landscaping back there. Your brother needs seclusion. With this house, that's what he'll get."

He helped her out of the car, then hurried toward a handsomely carved door. Bobbie hesitated. "Mr. Reid, this is the best you can show me?"

"You can't find anything better for the money. This one has comfortable furniture. And window screens. It even has indoor plumbing! Trust me, Miss McElroy. Your brother will love it!"

Officially it was the first day of spring, but by afternoon in Guadalajara it felt like early summer.

"Jim's coming?" Lester was pacing around the front room.

"Yes, and we aren't ready for him. Help me, Les. We need to bring one of the twin beds in here."

They had just assembled the bed near the front door when they heard the sound of a horn. Lester opened the door and rushed out.

Bobbie dropped an armload of bedding and ran after him. "Welcome to Guadalajara!" she called. "How was the drive?"

"Unbelievable!" Jim replied. "You were smart to avoid it. But isn't she a beaut?" He motioned toward the car.

Lester had been examining the car; he had a dirty streak across his forehead. When Jim passed him a rag, he wiped his hands. "She's a beaut!" he said and smiled.

"Four hundred smackers, but she's worth more!" Jim said. "We got a break because of the all-cash deal. She's Model A, of course. What do you think?" He looked at Bobbie.

"Marvelous!" she said and smiled.

Inside the house, Lester headed for the stairs. "Jim has to see my rooms first." He turned to make sure that Jim was following him. "Bobbie, you need to fix the bed."

She laid the sheets and blankets and put two pillows on Jim's bed. Afterwards, although she wanted to, she didn't go upstairs. She knew Les didn't want her there. He wants to surprise Jim,

she thought. She kicked off her shoes and stretched out on the bed she'd just made.

Lester opened the door to his bedroom and lifted a sleepy dog from the bed. "Yappo!" he said. "What do you think of him, Jim?" He sat on the floor and held Yappo on his lap.

Jim knelt beside them and stroked the short brown fur. At once the young dog licked Jim's hand and struggled to reach his face. Jim laughed. "I like him!" he said. "And I'll love him after he's had a bath. How much did you pay for Yappo?"

"Nada. Not one peso. The people at the hotel...wanted me to take him. He cried and yapped...all night long. That's why...I named him El Yappo." Lester spoke without stuttering.

Jim looked around the small room. It needed a fresh coat of whitewash. The ceiling was low and sloping. Its only redeeming feature was that French doors opened onto a balcony. Beyond it he saw trees and dense undergrowth.

"The rooms up here are my rooms. Mine and Yappo's. This one's for sleeping. The other one's...my workroom." Carrying the dog, Lester led the way to another small room.

"Is this where you'll put your new Victrola?"

"Did you get a radio, too? And my drawing pads?"

KALORAMA

"All the stuff on your list. We could bring it up right now! How about helping me unload the auto?" Jim waited, smiling, while Lester decided how to answer the question.

It took awhile to decide where to put things, especially the art supplies. Lester kept changing his mind. Finally Jim said, "Let's leave it this way. In a few days you'll know how to improve it."

Lester didn't answer. He was putting a record on the Victrola.

Jim went downstairs and looked around. He found Bobbie on the patio.

"How do you like the place?" She yawned and climbed out of the hammock.

"It'll do fine. No one could ask for a nicer patio. Or better weather!" He placed a rope on the large wrought iron table, then reached over to cut vines from a nearby lemon tree.

"Everything's been neglected," she said. "The hedge is jasmine, and those big red flowers are some kind of hibiscus. The real estate agent told me."

Jim looked around at the weeds invading the shrubbery and the citrus and other trees. "I like plants. It'll be fun to save these. Maybe Lester will lend a hand. He helped me unload the car—provided I'd make a leash for Yappo."

Bobbie laughed. "That sounds like the old Lester! Does be really need a leash?"

"He wants to take the dog along when we go out for supper. He wants carne tacos and Carta Blanca beer."

"He had them last night. Only we saved the beer for bedtime. Our nightcap. That's the easy way to get the medicine into him. I snuck it into his beer."

"I'm glad you told me," Jim said. "I'll use the nightcap method, too."

Bobbie dragged a wrought iron chair closer to the table. She watched while Jim braided hemp into a secure but gentle harness, then attached a generous length of rope.

"I'm glad my bed's in the front room," he said. "At night I'll block the door. He'll never get past me. Or make it through that briar patch out back."

"The agent called it a thicket."

"Well, that thicket makes my job easier. Les is too soft to hack his way out—especially at night. Of course, I hope he won't want to."

"Does he seem different to you? He actually helped me move some furniture! And he's not stuttering as much."

Jim gave her a sharp glance. "What other miracles are you expecting? I thought our goal was to give Les a vacation. One year in Mexico."

She didn't answer right away. She was trying to recognize the song Lester was playing. Then she

heard Rudy Valle singing the words. "I wanna be happy/but I won't be happy/'til I make you happy, too."

She gazed up at a cloudless, blue sky. "What you just said reminded me of Dr. Myers. He advised me to leave Lester in the hospital. Medical research will come to his rescue. Maybe I'm a fool to think I know what's best for my brother—and spend so much money this way."

"You care about Lester. And it's your money."

"It belongs to him, too. After our grandmother died, we sold the farm."

"I'll bet Lester's getting the lion's share. Our monthly allowance seems generous."

"Les needs more than good weather and this house. I'm hoping he can enjoy Guadalajara. Some parts of it."

"He's already asked me to drive him around. He wants to spot the best places for Yappo to run.

She smiled. "Lester found the dog. I'd never have thought of getting one. What kind do you think he is?"

"Mexican mutt—but worth his weight in gold. He loves Lester. Yappo will let me know if something's wrong."

She glanced at her wristwatch. "I'm forgetting about the taxicab. I'd better get my things together!"

"Don't you want us to drive you to the station?"

"I'll say goodbye to Les upstairs." She took another look around the sunny patio. "Jim, I don't

expect miracles, but I will pray for Lester. For both of you. Most of all, I'll pray that he'll enjoy being alive and want his years ahead. Whether this vacation changes him or not, my brother needed to come to Guadalajara. And I needed to bring him here."

When Bobbie glanced into the upstairs bedroom, she saw that Lester and Yappo were resting on the bed. Both seemed to be looking beyond the balcony to the clear blue sky. As soon as she said his name, Les sat up.

"Is it time for you to go, Bobbie?"

"I must get back to my job, but I wish I could stay here with you and Jim. And Yappo." She petted the sleepy little dog.

"Will you visit us?"

"As often as I can and I'll write letters. Jim will write back to me. Maybe you will, too."

"Jim and I are going out for supper, and Yappo's going with us. Jim promised to make him a leash."

"He made a fine one. Jim will be good to you. And you must be good to him." She gave Lester a hug and a kiss.

KALORAMA

From the hall window, Lester watched as Jim put the suitcase in the taxicab. He watched Bobbie and Jim shake hands. He kept watching until the taxi drove out of sight. Then he went into his workroom and looked everywhere. He went into his bedroom and looked everywhere. He and Yappo were safe. Jim was safe. Bobbie was safe, too. Everyone in the universe could be safe. He knew exactly what to do. He sat on the bed beside Yappo and, in his private language, told him the secrets.

APRIL

8

"Isn't it lovely!" From the doorway Letty Flagglar beamed at Mid and glanced around the refurbished dining hall. "I'm early, but I just can't wait another little minute."

"Come in, Letty!" Mid smiled at the well-to-do widow from Georgia, but kept working. She unfolded a white damask linen cloth and spread it over the long, center table. Smaller tables set with white linen, silverware, and cut-glass goblets lined the window wall.

The highly polished, dark walnut furniture gleamed against cream-colored wainscoting and pale blue wallpaper. Letty examined the

sideboard, which stood between the entrance and the door to the kitchen. Each drawer front was unique, a design of grapes and grape leaves or fruit and nuts. Letty ran her fingers over a cluster of walnuts.

"They don't carve like this anymore," she said. "I dearly love old things." She crossed the room to look at a buffet and a pair of corner cupboards. "It's simply charmin'! You made the perfect choice, Mid."

"I had nothing to do with it." Mid was placing linen napkins and silverware around the long table. "Everything in the old Hotel Columbia got sold at auction. Nels wanted the main dining room, so he kept bidding until he got it. All of it. His choice, Letty, not mine."

Letty hid a smile behind her chiffon dinner handkerchief. She'd heard the gossip about the Weigmanns' shouting match. "Mid honey, *c'est un fait accompli*. No point in frettin' 'bout it. Besides, this room's a treat for the eyes! I can hardly wait to plan a party for my lady friends."

Other boarders were arriving. Letty laid claim to the armchair at one end of the long table. With his large, strong right hand, Col. Smith steadied the chair for her. "Miss Letty, you look good enough to eat!" he said as he sat beside her. For this special occasion, he had enlivened his usual three-piece black suit with a new white shirt and a scarlet bow tie.

There was a buzz of excitement as ladies in dinner dresses and their escorts toured the room and chose places at the long table.

"Janet!" Letty called. "Come sit by me, sugar!"

A plain-faced young woman in powder-blue moire slipped into the designated chair. Two months earlier, Janet Wilson had taken the smallest bedroom on the third floor. The shy girl from Virginia and the voluble widow from Georgia had become friends. "Oh, Letty," she whispered, "I surely do admire your gown!"

Letty stood up and twirled. Scalloped panels of deep rose silk chiffon swirled around her short, firmly corseted figure. In the light of the chandelier, her crown of braids looked like brightly polished silver. "Thank you, Janet! I was hoping somebody would notice it. Bran' new!"

From across the table, Anna Menafee called, "Letty, I've just been waiting for the chance to tell you. You look marvelous!" Other voices joined in, assuring Letty that she had been admired. During the hubbub, Esther Lovell took the place beside Janet. And Walt Buchanan crossed the floor in three strides to claim the chair beside her.

"At last I get the chance to sit next to you," he told Esther. With a smile for the Menafees across the table, he helped Bobbie McElroy with her chair.

"Thanks, Walt," Bobbie said. "My word, but I'm grateful for this chance to change seats. I've heard Smitty's jokes so often that I'm telling them myself!"

Esther's laughter resembled phrases of music.

Walt smiled at her. "I've never heard you laugh before."

"Naughty of me to laugh, but I've had more than my share of the colonel's repertoire. I hope you don't go in for smutty jokes, Mr. Buchanan."

"Call me Walt, okay? I can't deny knowing some corkers. No way to avoid 'em in my business. Ladies' lingerie. But you'll get no traveling salesman jokes from me. That's a promise."

"And no tales out of school from me. So, what's left for us to talk about?" Esther's smiling brown eyes looked squarely into Walt's gray ones.

Bobbie had been watching and listening. "Esther, how's your dance club coming along?"

"Dance club?" Walt asked. "Don't you teach English?"

"And ballroom dancing after school. The principal suggested it when he learned how long I've studied dance. Over twenty years."

"Kids go for it?" Bobbie asked.

"Lots of girls. No boys."

Walt chuckled. "You'll get 'em. The dance club's a great idea."

"Esther, are you still going to Arthur Murray's?" Bobbie asked.

"Every Saturday afternoon. I wouldn't miss it for the world!" Esther blew a kiss to Nora, who had chosen to sit beside her Aunt Bobbie.

KALORAMA

"Where's Bill? Won't he be joining us?" Doug Menafee had been saving a place for his new friend.

"Pop expected to be back by now," Mid said. She glanced at her wristwatch. "He'd better step on the gas, or he'll end up with the leftovers."

At the head of the table, Nels got up and tapped his water goblet with a spoon. "Our gang's not all here. Bill had to help a sick buddy, and apparently the Haskells won't be with us. We can't wait for them any longer." He winked at Nora. "Somebody tells me she may faint from hunger, so my announcements must be fast and few." There was a ripple of laughter. "No doubt you've wondered about the extra tables. We've decided to open our dining hall to the public. If enough sign up for meals, we'll be able to enjoy rib roast of beef more often.

"Our new furnishings will be put to good use every morning. Except for Sunday pancakes, you'll help yourselves to the breakfast offerings. Breakfast is the only meal our college boys want here, and they've been begging for faster service.

"The Saturday night buffets will continue. All the rest of the week, Corinna will serve the main course and desserts. Everything else will be on the sideboard." Nels grinned. "Folks, what's the verdict? Do you approve of the changes?"

During the applause, Corinna appeared with a tray of appetizers. She was wearing a new black

sateen uniform with a white organdy apron, and her dimple was showing as she served the fresh fruit cups. Each had a topping of mint and the first strawberries of the season.

9

In her dream Lois Haskell was at home in Boston and lying on the mahogany spool bed where five generations of Haskells had made love to their wives. She was responding as Hugh made love to her.

She couldn't stay with him! Hands were pulling her, and a shrill voice was hurting her ear. It took a few seconds for her to realize that the hands and voice belonged to her six-year-old. Florence had wet-combed her hair around a crooked part. She had not done a good job of buttoning her dress.

"The clock didn't ring. Help me, Mama! I can't find my shoes. I don't dare to be late again." Florence crawled under her mother's bed.

Lois eased herself up against the headboard and reached for a glass on the nightstand. She drank

half its contents before she stood up and walked to the closet.

"You can wear these." She handed Florence a box containing a pair of patent leather Mary Jane's.

"Those dressed-up shoes hurt my toes."

"Well, what do you want to do? Stay home today."

"I can't! I'm behind." The child's eyes filled with tears. "Mama, I may be kept back in Miss Deming's room all next year."

Lois heard the bang of the door to the hall. She picked up the empty shoebox and the new tin of cookies. It felt empty, too. She crawled back into bed, but just as she was beginning to feel drowsy, someone rapped on the door. She expected to see Florence in the hall: instead she saw Corinna holding a wooden crate covered with newspaper.

"This here's what you ordered, Mrs. Haskell," she whispered. "Davey want one dollar more for each jug." She stepped into the Haskells' suite and placed the crate on the floor of their coat closet.

"He raised the price last time," Lois said.

Corinna avoided Mrs. Haskell's eyes. "I knows it, but Davey say you takes it or you leaves it."

Lois got her purse and counted out the money. "Is Florence still downstairs?"

"I ain't seen her since yesterday. Mrs. Weigmann sure felt bad when you missed the

fancy dinner party. She guessed you'd gone off with your uncle. We all seen Senator Shepard's big car out front."

After Corinna left, Lois went back to bed. But memories and the absence of memories kept her awake. She and Flo had missed the dinner party?

She remembered getting dressed for it. And sipping a glass of wine. She must have fallen asleep on top of the bed because that's where she'd been when Uncle Earl awakened her.

"Lillian and I hammered on your door. It wasn't locked, so we let ourselves in." Lois remembered how pink his face had looked.

Perched on the foot of the bed, Lillian had taken off her summer furs and held them on her lap. "We saw Florence downstairs. She told us where you were."

"Running your own speakeasy, Lois?" Earl motioned to a jug and wine glasses on the nightstand. At her nod, he'd fixed three small drinks.

Lillian tasted the amber-colored liquid. "What's it supposed to be?"

"Sh...sherry." Lois reached for her glass.

"Whatever it is, it packs a wallop," Earl said. "Lois, you'd better go easy on this stuff." He found a place to sit on the side of the bed.

Why are they here? Lois wondered. Why the party clothes? Doings on The Hill? Lillian had on diamond earbobs and shoulder clips. The raw silk dinner suit she wore had been featured in

Erlebocher's Christmas window. Lois had considered buying it to wear during the holidays in Boston.

Earl set his empty glass on the nightstand. "My dear, something's happened." He cleared his throat. "My God, how I wish your father was alive. He'd know just what to say."

Lois shivered. "Something's happened to Hugh!"

Earl reached for her hand. "Oh, Lois, you poor, dear child! No, Hugh's not hurt." He took a newspaper clipping from his breast pocket and handed it to her. "Maybe you ought to see for yourself."

He pointed to the picture of Hugh Henry Haskell V and his bride. "A photographer on *The Globe* spotted them at City Hall. Do you know her, Lois?"

Lois shook her head. She had met only a few of Hugh's lady friends. This attractive brunette was a stranger. Lois tried to control her trembling grasp on the clipping. She stared at Hugh's handsome, smiling mouth.

Lillian adjusted her furs and put on white doeskin gloves. "She's a nurse. Not Beacon Hill or anything else Gloria Haskell wants for her son. Hugh hadn't breathed a word of this to any of us."

When they'd gone, Lois studied the newspaper picture of Hugh's young wife. Tall girl, the athletic type. Her eyes kept filling with tears, making it impossible to see clearly. The crying had gone on

so long that even now it hurt to swallow. She had vague memories of scolding Florence and ordering her to bed. What else? She could not remember another thing.

It was after eleven when Lois added the last of her daytime suits to the pile on the floor. Like the others, it was at least one size too large. The only thing left to try had never been unpacked. In the steamer trunk she also found Florence's school shoes. Why on earth had she put them there?

The mirror on the closet door confirmed what she'd suspected. The blue faille suit fit well, but it was definitely passé. It would have to do if she were to get to Adams Elementary School before noon.

"Lois, you are showing your age," she told herself. "Every minute of thirty-four."

She'd hoped to leave the house without being noticed, but just as she approached the front door, Mildred Weigmann walked in. She was wearing a new shantung outfit.

"That shade of apple green is wonderful with your hair, Mid!" Lois said.

"I hope Nels likes it. Woodies slashed prices on coats and suits. The windows along F Street are featuring organdy. Crazy, isn't it? Summer clothes before we're really enjoying spring." She set several boxes on the hall table and pulled off her cloche

hat and gloves. "Will you be with us for dinner tonight?"

"Yes, and I'm sorry about last evening."

"It was quite a party—roast beef with all the trimmings. Too bad you and Flo had to miss it."

Lois opened the front door. "I must run. Florence forgot her lunch money again, and her shoes don't fit." Her voice faltered. She had seen Mid's expression change. The look of pity was fleeting but unmistakable.

Lois hurried along the school's quiet corridors. She knew the way to the first grade classroom. But could she get there in time? She wasn't up to searching for Florence in the noisy, crowded lunchroom. As she approached the rear of the building, she became aware of odors—canned string beans, boiled milk, and Lysol. The smell of American public schools.

Florence was sitting on the floor outside Miss Deming's closed door.

Lois knelt beside her. "What's going on?" she whispered. "Why aren't you with the other children?"

"My toes hurt, and I couldn't count the rabbits."

"Where are your patent leathers?" Lois helped her put on the school shoes.

"Miss Deming hid them in the closet." The noon bell rang, and Flo got out of the way of the door. Orderly lines of children soon filled the hall.

"Mama, can I eat lunch today?" She gave her mother a tear-stained ditto sheet. After receiving her lunch money, she squeezed into a line of little bodies. Miss Deming walked behind them.

Lois caught up with her. "Miss Deming, I must speak with you! Do you remember me? I'm Florence's mother."

Miss Deming motioned for a monitor to take charge of the line. "It'll have to be quick, Mrs. Haskell. I wish you'd made an after-school appointment."

She led the way to her classroom, unlocked the door, and hurried to her desk. Lois pulled up a student chair and sat beside her.

Already the teacher had consulted her grade book. "We have a bumper crop of first graders. It's all I can do to teach the class. I cannot meet the needs of forty-two individuals."

"Florence seems to think she's failing. Why was she sitting in the hall? Where are her shoes?"

Lois watched the middle-aged teacher walk to the closet. About an inch of pink petticoat hung unevenly in back, beneath her brown pleated skirt.

Miss Deming handed her the patent leathers. "I do not permit shoe passing in my classroom." Her mouth became a long, thin line. She was rocking slightly as she stared down at Lois.

"Was Florence doing that? What's shoe passing?"

The teacher sat at the desk. "She never did own up to it, but I know all about that little game. I'd been watching her. I keep an eye on all the youngsters who may be with me again next year."

"What was she doing wrong?"

"I stopped her just in time. She'd already taken off one shoe. If I hadn't caught her, she'd have passed it to another student. He'd pass his shoe, and pretty soon every shoe would be circulating around the room. Sometimes we can't find all of them. Imagine how our parents like that!" Furrows appeared between Miss Deming's neatly drawn, black eyebrows.

Lois looked down at the wrinkled paper Florence had given her. The ditto machine had misprinted. No one could have counted the rabbits.

"Miss Deming, look at this! You can see why Florence wasn't doing her sums. And I know why she took off her shoe. I'd misplaced the pair for school. These patent leathers pinch her toes."

The teacher's eyes widened as she examined the worksheet. "Why didn't she show me? Or explain about her toes?"

"I guess she's a little uncomfortable around you. Neither of us feels at home here. We both miss Boston."

"The child's afraid of me. And I've misjudged her." She again checked the grade book. "But I am

not mistaken about her record. She came with deficiencies, and she's done nothing but add to the list. Florence is not ready for the second grade."

"Can't you get her ready? Or recommend a tutor?"

Miss Deming led the way to the hall. "No child could make up a year's work in the time that's left. Next fall we'll find a good tutor. Meanwhile do what you can. At least keep a tight rein on your daughter. She's too easily distracted and led astray. I know what I'm talking about, Mrs. Haskell. I've taught a good many little girls like Florence."

Nobody else was in the entrance hall at Kalorama. Lois went into the telephone room and placed a call to her former mother-in-law.

"Oh, Lois, I'm so glad it's you. My dear, you have no idea how much I've wanted to call you, but the phone's been ringing all morning. Everybody's asking about Hugh and that nurse. You do know what he's done?"

"Uncle Earl told me. But that's not why I've called."

"Oh, what am I to do? I don't understand my son. I've never understood him. Why did he insist on medicine? Everybody knows that Haskells aren't doctors. Haskells are bankers. The only time Hugh ever pleased me was when he married you.

For once in his life he followed my advice. The two of you have everything in common—the only kind of marriage that wears well."

Lois listened while Hugh's mother wept. She could easily picture Gloria Haskell, her lips close to the mouthpiece, but with the earphone at some distance from the wave covering her ear. Her long, dark hair was always carefully pinned into a chignon at the nape of her neck. Hugh had the same heavy hair and the same large, gray eyes.

"Please, Mother Haskell, don't cry. You did all you could to keep us together, and I love you for trying. What's happened is my fault as well as his. If I hadn't gone to the lawyer, we'd still be married. But I couldn't take it anymore—feeling humiliated and jealous. And angry. I was fed up with friends telling me about his latest cutie…"

Between sobs Gloria Haskell said, "Every night I pray that Hugh will honor his marriage vows and do right by his family. Oh, Lois, what a dreadful Christmas we had!"

Lois waited for her mother-in-law to regain control of herself. The weeping became so stormy that Gloria dropped the receiver. When she picked it up, she said, "I can't talk now. In a few minutes?"

"I'll wait by the phone."

Lois sat farther back in the armchair and looked out the window. Hundreds of white and yellow daffodils were in bloom near the carriage house, but

she wasn't thinking about springtime. She was remembering the Christmas holidays.

As soon as she'd arrived in Boston, she'd prepared to make a surprise visit to Hugh. With Gloria's help, she'd found the perfect outfit—Chanel's winter white wool. The following afternoon she'd gone directly from the beauty salon to Hugh's office.

The timing could not have been better. Visiting hours were over, and his long-time receptionist was just leaving for the day. "You're looking very festive, Mrs. Haskell!" she said. "The doctor's at his desk."

Just beyond the waiting room was the washroom, and Lois went in to use the mirror. She smiled at her reflection. There was no need to add lipstick or change a thing. Still smiling, she went down the hall to the last room. Through the open door she saw Hugh at his desk. As she walked toward him, she called, "Merry Christmas!"

She had succeeded in surprising him. He stared at her for what felt like a long time, but there was no look of pleasure on his handsome face. "Why are you here?" he asked. "The final divorce papers will arrive any day now."

She noticed an unfamiliar touch of white in his sideburns and thought, Hugh will be forty on his next birthday. She moved to his side of the desk. "You and I belong together. Let's burn the damn papers and give ourselves another honeymoon!

Darling, I love you more than ever." She touched his cheek.

He stood, took her by the hand, and escorted her back to the empty waiting room. "Lois, it's all over. I don't love you. Maybe I never did. I wish to God you'd divorced me years ago!"

She felt as if he'd knocked the breath out of her. She couldn't utter a word. Or decide what to say. Her best thoughts had gone into letters she'd sent him. She'd counted on her letters. And on Gloria.

"What about Florence?" she whispered.

"By law she's all yours." He gave a wry smile. "My only duty is to safeguard the trust funds and securities."

Hugh's eyes seemed to be appraising her. "You'll marry well. Probably with Mother's help. Good luck to you, Lois."

She felt herself being led across the foyer of the medical building. The black and white tiles looked damp, and there was the strong odor of carbolic acid. Then she'd been alone, outside in the cold air.

The telephone rang, and Lois heard Gloria Haskell's voice the moment she lifted the receiver.

"Mother Haskell, I need your help. For Florence."

There was a sharp intake of breath. "Is she sick?"

"No, nothing like that, but I've had a talk with her teacher. Florence has to repeat the first grade.

But not here. Washington's not the right place for her. I want her in a private school near Boston."

"Boarding school? But, Lois, the child's so young!"

"She'll be seven. I was six when Father sent me to Lucerne. What Florence needs is you, Mother Haskell. She needs your firm grip on her. And she needs her father."

"I despised boarding school. Lois, are you certain you want to do this?"

"I can't give her what she needs. Not now. It's as though I can't think of anyone but Hugh. Oh, Mother Haskell, please help us!"

"It seems that I have no other choice." Gloria Haskell paused. "I guess I should start with Libby Parkhurst. God knows, she's spent a fortune on private schools. Don't worry, Lois. I'll find the right place for my grandchild. Please give the little darling my love."

"Call me? We'll be here until the Senate adjourns. Then we'll be in Chatham with Uncle Earl and Lillian. Two months at the Cape should do wonders for my poor baby. After that, she'll be ready for a new school. And new friends—the right sort. By fall I may feel better, too. Thank you, Mother Haskell."

Lois began the climb to the second floor. She could hardly wait to strip off the faille suit. It belonged in the trash room, along with her other discards. Tomorrow she'd go to Arden's for a smart

new shingle. And to Erlebocher's for clothes—the best of their spring collection. The path ahead looked lonely. But she'd take it one-step-at-a-time. For now, she needed to change into her peignoir and slippers. And relax with a big, stiff drink.

10

On Sundays Mid and her father always did the breakfast dishes. Bill washed and rinsed. Mid dried and stored. One china cupboard covered most of the wall beside the door to the hall. Twenty feet across the kitchen, two smaller cupboards flanked the pantry door. Mid used them all, as well as the plate rack that circled the room.

"We're taking Nora to the Fox," Mid said. "Want to go along?" She set the last stack of plates in his dishpan.

Bill gave his daughter a blank look. "What?"

"Nora's birthday. Do you want to go downtown with us? It's Astaire and Rogers."

"Nora's birthday! Today?"

"No, Dad, it's tomorrow. A school day. So we're taking her to the matinee today. She wants to see a stage show."

"I forgot Nora's birthday." He dried his hands on a tea towel.

Mid stared at her father. All her life he'd insisted on tea towels for dishes, roller towels for hands. She took another look at his neatly combed hair and carefully rolled shirtsleeves. Everything about him seemed to be all right except for the way he was acting.

Bill ignored the plates and scoured a frying pan.

"Nels got her the baby doll she wanted for Christmas," Mid said. "Life-sized in a bassinet—bedding, bottles, layette. No wonder Woodies still had it. I could buy her a nice spring coat for less."

Bill set the pan in rinse water. "I don't have enough in my bag."

Nora's birthdays always featured Daddy Bill's grab bag. This year she was due eight grabs from his collection of oddities.

"What's going on, Dad?"

"What do you mean?"

"You seem distracted. What's wrong?"

"I'm worried about Eddie." The lines on both sides of Bill's mouth deepened. "He says he's feeling somewhat better, but he can't fool me. The pain's coming more often, and it's worse."

"Oh, poor, dear Eddie. How can I help?" After an uncomfortable silence, she said, "Want to see what I got for Nora?"

Bill dried his hands on a roller towel before examining the maroon leather book. The silhouette of a

little girl of long ago had been embossed on its cover. About five inches square, the book had lined, gilt-edged pages.

He turned the small brass key in its lock. "Nora will enjoy keeping a diary. It's right up her alley."

"I wanted to get her a fountain pen, too. She has to have one for the third grade. But Nels went overboard on that doll."

"I'll get the pen. A Parker or a Shaeffer." Bill returned the diary and gave his daughter a kiss. "But no matinee for me today. Eddie wants to see the cherry blossoms. If he's up to it, I'll drive him around the Tidal Basin."

"Will they let him go?"

"Sure, if he wants to. Most days he just wants to stay put. And talk. Eddie's dredging up bits of our childhood. It gives us both a laugh."

"Nels thinks it's cancer."

Bill nodded. "They tell me to pray." Bill ran the dish mop around and around a large bowl. "Praying is what they do best over there."

11

Walter Buchanan pocketed his keys and put on his wristwatch. Almost two. Accounts and invoices had taken up too much of his Sunday. But for once the remaining hours belonged to him. His daughter had "a heavy date."

That was about all Vera could tell him. She'd never met the boy—knew nothing about him. "That's Skee's business, Walt. Keep your big nose out of it." As usual, Vera had hung up on him.

Walt checked his wallet. Enough for gas and a bite to eat. Vera didn't want his advice, but she sure did want his money, every cent the law allowed. He adjusted the brim of his fedora and opened the door to the hall.

"Walt!" Esther Lovell ran toward him. Her large brown eyes looked unhappy.

"What's wrong, Esther?"

"Can you drive Pixie to the vet?"

"Of course. What's the matter with her?"

Instead of answering, Esther ran down the stairs. Walt followed her all the way to the back yard.

"I was putting my bike away when I heard whimpers." She showed him where Pixie lay motionless behind the carriage house. "Is she still alive?"

Walt touched Pixie's tan fur and with gentle fingers examined her small body. "She's unconscious. Good thing, too. Both hind legs are broken." He felt again along Pixie's spine. "I'm afraid her back's broken, too. Ayres must have used a club on her. Did you call the S.P.C.A.?"

"They're out on other calls. No telling when they'd get here."

"There's a vet on Wisconsin Avenue." Walt caught Esther's hand. "No, don't lift her. We need something stiff to use as a pallet."

He ran into the carriage house and came back with a piece of beaverboard. "Let's put her on the front seat—wedged between us."

"She's breathing funny. What does that mean?"

"Let's go!"

Neither of them spoke until they reached Wisconsin Avenue.

"This is good of you, Walt." Esther's voice sounded weepy.

"Glad to do it. But what if I'd already left? I usually spend Sunday afternoon with my kid."

"I don't know. Corinna expects the Weigmanns home by five. But think of Nora! What would this do to her?"

"It's her birthday," Walt said. "Some present this would be." He double-parked outside the Pet and Vet. "Esther, get somebody. Hurry!"

Within seconds, she was back. "Nobody's around. The sign says Closed until Four. Where's the nearest vet?"

"We can't waste time looking for one. Let's find a drug store. We can use their telephone directory."

They had driven several long blocks before spotting Walgreens. It was at a busy intersection.

"No place to park," Walt said. "You go in. I'll drive around the block."

He waited until he saw Esther entering the drug store. Then he checked Pixie. Her breath was unpleasant, but the board beneath her was clean and dry. At his touch Pixie did not open her eyes. Driving slowly, Walt began to circle the block.

He wondered what Skee was doing. Heavy date. The boy couldn't have much spending money. Maybe they were renting bikes and riding around the Tidal Basin. The cherry trees would be spectacular today! Walt smiled. That was the afternoon he'd planned for Skee. But she seldom liked his plans. Last Sunday, he'd been primed to

see the latest arrivals at the zoo. Skee wanted to see a movie. Her favorites starred long-suffering females he could barely stand.

He kept circling the block. Finally he caught sight of Esther. She waved and ran to the car.

"Which one?" She handed him a column torn from the directory.

"Macomb Street," Walt decided and returned the list. He saw her put it in a pocket of her plaid skirt. "I like the things you wear," he said. At the first break in traffic, he joined the steady stream of cars.

Walt glanced at Esther and saw that her face was pink. It had been a long time since he'd seen anyone blush. It made Esther look very young. And very sweet.

"Thanks. I bought this skirt and tam in Scotland. Along with some other plaids."

"I especially like that blue floaty dress you wear to Arthur Murray's. Were you surprised when I joined the class?"

She smiled. "You're an excellent dancer, Walt."

"I used to be pretty good, but I don't know any of the new steps."

"Want me to show you? Maybe after class?"

"What a swell idea!"

Esther looked at Pixie. "Oh, Walt, I don't think she's breathing!"

Walt pulled into a no-parking zone and checked Pixie "She's gone." He sighed. "Well,

Ayres can't hurt her anymore. By God, I'd like to knock that guy's block off!" Walt pulled the handkerchief from his breast pocket and handed it to Esther. "Where do you want to take her? I have to move the car."

Tears were running down Esther's face. She cradled Pixie in her arms. "Let's go home," she said.

"It's probably where she'd like to be. There's a shovel in the carriage house. You pick a nice spot, and I'll dig the hole."

Esther blew her nose. "Pixie liked to sleep under the hawthornes. But we won't tell Nora where she is. Let's keep all of this to ourselves."

"Our secret."

Esther held Pixie on her lap and tried to sing "In the Sweet Bye and Bye." In her soft, rich contralto she sang the words she knew and hummed the rest. Mostly she wept.

After a while, Walt lifted the board out of the way and reached for her hand. They rode hand-in-hand until he had to park the car.

MAY

12

Corinna ran across the lobby toward the front doors of the Gayety Theatre. Only one of the wall sconces was lit although it was early morning and still dark outside. Above the center door the face of the clock gleamed white against the wine-red wallpaper. Ten minutes to catch her trolley.

The Ninth Street lights were on. Outside the big church at the corner drab figures were lining up for free bread and coffee. The soup kitchen never opened before seven. Those folks had a mighty long while to wait.

Boarding the trolley, she gave the conductor a smile that showed off her dimple. "Gotta get me some shuteye, Mr. Russell. Don't you be forgetting my wake-up call."

"I ain't fixing to forget you, Miz Watts. Why you be treating us to that pretty hat this morning?"

"Henny's birthday!" Smiling, she moved to the rear of the streetcar and chose a seat well beyond the three other passengers. All of them looked asleep. Carefully, she wedged her handbag between herself and the window wall and closed her eyes. She could not relax.

Rubbing the back of her neck felt good, but it didn't make her sleepy. What she really wanted was to pull off her shoes, but if she did, she'd never get them back on her swollen feet. She'd end up walking three long blocks in her only good pair of stockings. Best take her mind off her feet and hands and the ache that burned between her shoulder blades. "Think about Henny, ' she told herself. "Forty today. Sure don't act his age!"

Nobody at Kalorama knew about her job at the bur-le-que. "Ain't none of their business," she muttered. They didn't know Henny either. She'd planned to ask the missus for time off—maybe the whole morning. But Henny landed the job on the coal wagon. Day work and steady pay. Right after the birthday treats, she'd go across town for her usual full day of work. Extra full. She had to help out at the colonel's poker party.

KALORAMA

Henny's treats? She'd stop by the All-Nite. For his breakfast, her man was getting a nice piece of fried ham, eggs over light, grits, and a bowl of red-eye gravy. Hot biscuits, too! But first the kiss—soft and slow just like he want it. After that? Jack Daniels. Good thing she spotted the paper bag in the balcony. Enough left for a couple big swigs.

By the time he see the feast, Henry be feeling real tickled—laughing and showing all his pretty teeth. How he do when he see the big surprise? "He sure ain't 'specting nothing like this!" Tingles cold but sweet made her shiver. She felt inside her handbag. It was there. Safe.

Too dark outside to see much, but the window glass gave a view of her own tired face. No time to doll herself up. Not that The Gayety was hard to clean. It was an easy job—except for the lobby. She'd been there—rubbing a little polish on the gilt nudes—when Mr. Jacoby came looking for her. "Corinna, it's double duty for you tonight. Marie Hall quit on me." He paid her Marie's dollar, too.

What a night! Sweeping—dumping—checking the clock. Lick and promise jobs everywhere. But oh my soul, them bathrooms! Guys and Dolls. Afterwards the quick change into her print dress and new hat. Pink felt with a veil.

She arched her back and stretched her legs. "Girl, why you ain't sleepy?" she asked herself. "Something worrying your mind?" She pressed her

palms together and bent her head. In a voice that only God could hear, she said, "Thank You for what You done tonight. But I ain't sure what You want me to do. Dear Lord, I need a sign."

The sign did not come. She tried to relax and drift off to sleep, but something kept its hold on her. Working too hard? This evening the clock in the lobby had pushed her along, faster and faster. "Just sweep, flush, and wipe," she'd told herself. "If you ain't done with Dolls in fifteen minutes, you ain't catching your trolley." But the mirror looked ugly—dirty words in purple-red lipstick. A little ammonia on the rag, a few good wipes, and the words were gone. Dusting the sides and bottom of the gilt frame made the top look gray. She stretched up and over the counter and sink.

The feather duster had flicked something that hit the drainpipe with a ping. She couldn't see what it was until she got down on her knees. Near the pipe was a small, shiny object. Gold with three stones. Even before she picked it up, she knew the ring was valuable. The stones looked like diamonds. There was nothing inside the band except 18k. She eased the ring over the knuckles of her left pinkie. "Lord, thank You for letting me find it."

Again she felt inside her handbag. Wrapped in toilet paper, the ring filled the pocket intended for a mirror. She moved closer to the window and rested her arm on top of her bag. "Dear Father in

Heaven, does you want for Henny and me to have it?" She stared at her knuckles, whitening against the light brown of her clenched hands. "I can't hear you, Lord. The onliest thing strong in my mind is Henny." She shivered. "Is that the sign?"

Henny got to know everything about tonight— just like he seen it all for himself. He got to feel it, too. The wonder of God's love.

She pictured the ring on his big, pink-brown palm. Henny smiling and knowing what to do. She let out a deep breath. The buzzing in her ears got louder, like somebody whispering, like Henny sweet-talking. She tried to hear the words. But sleep was carrying her away.

Mid glanced at the clock. Five-thirty a.m. She'd spent the night listening for Nels and worrying about the bills. After a weary yawn, she got out of bed.

His old smoking jacket lay on the floor. Nels had aimed for the bedside chair but missed. For some reason, that had ended their argument. He'd slammed the front door on his way out of the house.

She smoothed the silk and wool jacket over a padded hangar. Against the worn lining, the label looked bright. Saville Row. The wardrobe closet smelled of lavender that Nels' grandmother had

kept there many years ago. His boyhood had been happy only because of her. He'd spent every holiday and most weekends at Grandy's house.

"Grandy's things will look fine in this room," Nels had said. "They're mahogany and rosewood. Massive pieces. They need this twelve-foot ceiling. And the fleur-de-lis wallpaper will do very well."

She had protested. The gold-on-white paper had been on the walls for thirty years. But he'd been right. Their bed-sitting room was beautiful. No one would ever guess that room had been intended for formal dining.

She adjusted the fringed window shades. Four tall windows gave a view of the lawn, refreshed by last night's shower. Drops of water falling from trees and shrubs glistened in the early morning light.

Nels had changed jackets, but he'd forgotten to take his raincoat or umbrella. He'd been too angry to notice the rain.

The whole thing had been her fault. She should have confessed about the loveseat during dinner. Nels hated quarrelling in public, so he'd have taken the bad news quietly. Instead, she'd been in bed, nearly asleep, when he'd entered their bedroom and spotted the sofa. Stripped of upholstery fabric, it looked bad.

"What happened?" he'd demanded.

"I tried to clean it. The material sort of dissolved."

KALORAMA

"Why didn't you ask me first? You know how I feel about Grandy's things." His face had looked flushed and contorted. As if he were about to yell—or cry.

"It never occurred to me to ask your permission."

"Nothing's left of the fabric. No way to match it. That thought never occurred to you either, did it?"

She'd felt her cheeks getting warm, but managed to keep her voice cool and steady. "Check underneath."

Carefully he'd laid the piece on its side. "You're right. Lots of fabric! That Georgetown shop may have something similar. Or know how to get it."

After setting the sofa upright, he'd sat in the center of it. "Sorry I sounded off like that. From start to finish, it's been a hell of a day. The roofers called. They want $200 before repairing the damage."

"To fix that little leak?"

"$200 up front. More when they finish. The roof is in worse shape than I thought. Where's that cash coming from? I'm dunning everybody who owes us. So far, no soap."

"Buchanan? He's never been so late before."

Nels shrugged. "This afternoon I got into a knock-down, drag-out argument over the grocery account. No deliveries unless I paid up. I had to kite a check. Where's that money coming from? Tomorrow I have to deposit it in the bank."

"I'll get it from Pop."

"Your father can't bail us out. Not this time. He's barely keeping his own head above water. He's been paying some of Eddie's bills. Didn't you know?"

Pop had never discussed money problems with her. "I might have guessed. Eddie has no family. Pop and I are all he has." Brushing away sudden tears, she got out of bed and went over to Nels. "Do you have any idea how this makes me feel? We can't fix the leak, we can't pay the grocer, we can't help Uncle Eddie. Why are we in this fix? We had plenty of money in our savings account. What happened to it?" She grabbed the lapels of his jacket and forced him to look at her. "You spent it on dining room furniture."

Without another word, he'd changed jackets and left.

After making the bed, she draped an afghan over the loveseat. It would wait its turn. When they did have money to spend on it, Nels would insist on doing it Grandy's way. Traditional colors and patterns. Anything modern looked cheap to Nels—not that he'd use that word. "Overstated" was what he'd probably say.

During their courtship he'd disliked a good many of her outfits. "Mildred Norris, the only taste you have is in your mouth," he'd said with a laugh. She'd laughed with him. But later, alone, she'd cried.

KALORAMA

He'd fallen for her anyway, despite her yen for Hollywood fashions. And her grammar. Mid grinned. Her grammar must have improved over the years. Nels hadn't played English teacher for a long while.

It was time to wash and dress. While the tub filled, she checked on Nora. Always a good sleeper, the child did not awaken as Mid selected the clothes for school. The alarm clock on the desk ticked loudly. She set it so it would ring in about an hour.

The warm bath water made her feel sleepy. She grabbed the long-handled brush and vigorously scrubbed her back. Today she'd wear the green twill jumper. Corinna had done a nice job of pressing it. The girl was a hard worker—willing to put in long days. Like this one. Smitty's poker game was tonight. Would Nels remember? She whispered, "Oh God, please keep him safe. Bring him home to Nora and me."

"Corinna? It's past eight. Aren't you supposed to be helping out upstairs?" Mid was cutting a large pan of butterscotch brownies into squares.

"The colonel want a bridge table. Okay for me to get him one?"

"Yes, of course, but why does he need it? It's a poker party."

"Ain't no place to set out the food. He got guns all over his parlor table."

"He wants to sell them. He put ads in all the papers so that means you and I will be running back and forth to the telephone." Mid handed her a plate of brownies. "Save two of these for yourself. Is he serving his usual smelly cheese and crackers?"

Corinna wrinkled her nose. "He sent me up the street for 'em. Awful smelly cheese."

"Well, maybe Menafee and Buchanan will enjoy it. My men won't touch that stuff."

"Me neither—even if it do come from Avignon Fears."

"Frères. It means brothers. Wait a minute, Corinna." Mid went into the pantry. When she returned, she said, "Put it near the crackers." It was a small dish of peanut butter. "Is my husband up there?"

Corinna had noticed the puffy redness of Mid Weigmann's eyes. She'd spotted the wet handkerchief, too. "No m'am, I ain't seen him all day."

But when Corinna got back to the colonel's suite, Nels Weigmann met her at the door. He had on his good suit and the shirt she'd ironed earlier that day.

"You have too much to carry," he said. With a smile, he took the card table from her and set it up near the fireplace. After lighting a cigarette, he joined his father-in-law and Douglas Menafee. They were looking at the pistols on the parlor table.

KALORAMA

"This one's my prize," Col. Smith said. Without looking, Corinna knew that the colonel was the speaker. He had a deep voice and a kind of smiley way of talking like some white folks down home. "My father bought this Derringer in 1855."

"May I take a look? It must be one of the first. I'd bet it's worth quite a bit by now."

Corinna spread a linen cloth over the card table. She recognized Mr. Menafee's voice.

"You'd win the bet, Doug. That piece ought to bring top dollar. So will this revolver. Single action. Believe it or not, I won it in a poker game. It dates back to 1873."

"I betcha I can date this baby," Nels Weigmann said. "German Luger 1914. I own one of these myself." He pulled a pack of Old Golds from his breast pocket. "Any chance of a highball, Smitty?"

Corinna watched while the glasses were filled. It would be her job to keep them filled. The colonel fixed his usual bourbon and water. The others took scotch and soda. All but Mr. Norris. He was still examining a gun.

"That's my best Colt Automatic," the colonel told him. "Not too pricey. If you're interested, Bill, I'll make you a sweet deal."

Corinna carried a tray to Bill Norris. It held a tall drink and a dish of nuts.

"Rye and water?" he asked.

"Yes sir, I fix it like you always takes it."

KALORAMA

He put down the pistol and accepted the drink. Smiling, he carried the dish to the others now comfortably seated on the leather sofa and easy chairs.

"Walt expects to get here by eight-thirty," the colonel said. "Just the five of us tonight." He signaled that the nut dish was empty.

She carried it to the bathroom. Once a taproom, it had an icebox and storage cupboards. She filled the crystal dish with the last of the almonds. "I got to chip more ice," she reminded herself. "But first the missus need to know her man come home." She went downstairs to tell Mid.

By the time she got back, the colonel was telling one of his nasty jokes. She placed the crystal dish where he could reach it. Before helping himself to the nuts, he tapped his empty glass. "Fix me up, gal." His face was pink from laughing.

The makings for drinks and food were nearby on the card table. As soon as he received his fresh highball, the colonel waved Corinna away. "Stand your post!" he said.

Within easy view of the poker table was a tall radiator. With her back against it, she could ease her knees and feet. There'd be long waits between signals. "Stop whining, girl," she muttered. "You getting paid. A dollar maybe! Besides, you ain't all that weary."

She'd had a nap today—after lunch, while the missus was upstairs. No big ironing job today, just

a couple shirts and the fancy uniform she wore to parties. A fine sleep in the kitchen rocker 'til the girls be home from school and she got to fix their graham crackers and milk.

Mr. Buchanan showed up while she was serving drinks. All he wanted was ice and ginger ale. "I'm not much of a drinker, Corinna," he said. "This will do me for the evening." His gray eyes smiled at her, and she smiled back. Before choosing a seat, he handed an envelope to Nels Weigmann, saying he was sorry for the delay.

She liked Mr. Buchanan. She did not like his ex-wife—calling up at breakfast time—always putting colored folks down. Why he take up with white trash the likes of her? But he got it good now. Sweet on the school teacher. Sure look like Miss Lovell be mighty sweet on him. Corinna chuckled. "Oh my soul, what I knows 'bout them!"

"Clean ashtrays, Corinna!" Col. Smith called.

"Smitty, do you subscribe to the *Times?*" Mr. Norris reached for the New York paper on the coffee table.

"My nephew left it when he came to thank me for the graduation check. " The colonel set aside his empty glass.

"V.M.I.?" Nels Weigmann asked.

"Georgetown. The lad wants to be a lawyer."

"I hope he gets the chance. I'd trained for field engineering. Uncle Sam changed my plans."

Bill Norris held the paper so they could all see the headline, MUSSOLINI WARNS POWERS TO LEAVE ETHIOPIA TO ITALY. "I don't like the look of this."

"I don't either," Doug Menafee said. "The Germans are conscripting an army of 500,000. It's on the front page of the *Baltimore Sun*."

"The *Star* carried the same story," Mr. Buchanan said. "Hitler's violating the Versailles treaty. The League's going to apply sanctions if they have to."

"The League? Nothin' but a bunch of Fancy Dan's. They can't stop Hitler." The colonel glanced at his wristwatch. "It's close to nine. How about some poker?" On his way to the gaming table, he selected a large brownie.

Corinna didn't understand poker. Henny was smart about cards, but he got no time or money for them. Down home he used to tell 'bout winning a big pot. Fifty dollars! She ain't never figured out how he won it.

"Draw poker," Col. Smith announced as he lit his cigar.

Mr. Buchanan looked at Nels Weigmann. "The pot's the limit?"

"Yep, and the blue chip's a quarter."

Corinna gave up trying to follow their strange, fast talk. She let her thoughts turn to Henny. He sure been talking fast this morning. 'Specially about the ring. Over and over she had to tell him how it

KALORAMA

happened. And 'bout her prayers. "What God want for me to do? Put it in the lost and found?" Henny laughed when she said that. "Iffen you do, Cory, you is one big fool. Lost and found just mean you lost and Jacoby found." Henny had no sorry feelings for the lady who lost her fine ring. "She done it to herself. Losers weepers, finders keepers." On the tip of his finger, the ring fit like a thimble. "It be safe with me." He put the ring deep inside a pocket of his wallet.

"Supposin' the police...?"

"Ain't gonna be no police. If Jacoby ask, all you say is you don't know what happen to no ring. And that be the truth 'cause I ain't telling you. All you gonna know is what we get for it."

"What you think we gonna get?"

"All's I can. Cory, I know who to see."

"Henny, what we gonna do with all that money?" She knew the answer, but she loved hearing it.

"It gonna help us go back home to stay."

She closed her eyes and let her mind fill up with memories. Alfalfa warm in the sunshine and smelling sweet. Cotton covering the fields like snow. Mam's hollyhocks most as tall as Henny.

"Corinna!" Col. Smith called. "Wake up, gal!" He put down his cards and pounded the table. For a one-armed man, he made a lot of noise.

She hurried to replace ashtrays and drinks.

Nels Weigmann was stacking up a whole lot of chips. "You almost got me that time, Smitty. If I hadn't drawn that..."

"Quit the post mortems. Deal me some winners, Nels!" The colonel had big stacks of chips, too. As soon as he saw his new cards, he raised the bet.

Mr. Buchanan stood up. "That's too rich for my blood. Thanks, Smitty, but I'm out of the game." He gave Corinna his empty glass. "See you in the morning."

"Yes sir, Mr. Buchanan."

The refreshment table was ready, except for ice. Corinna hurried to get it. Taking careful aim with the pick, she broke off a chunk that nearly filled the small sink behind the bar. She chipped enough ice to fill the bucket and drank a glass of ice water. After that, she treated herself to brownies.

On the way back to the game, she detoured into the colonel's bedroom. The hands on his bedside clock pointed to eleven. Could she get to the Gayety by midnight?

The living room was quiet. Everybody seemed to be waiting for something to happen. The colonel's face was red, his bow tie crooked, white hair on end. He looked like he wanted to throw pitchforks at somebody.

Mr. Menafee took off his eyeglasses and rubbed the pinch marks on his nose. Then he spread his cards so everybody could see them. "Royal flush, gentlemen. Read 'em and weep."

"By God, Doug, you sure had me fooled!" Nels Weigmann said. He clapped Menafee on the shoulder.

Bill Norris grinned at his friend from Baltimore. "I thought bridge was your game. Doug, you have the classiest poker face I ever saw!" Menafee smiled, but he did not look up. He was counting chips.

"You be wanting a fresh drink, Col. Smith?"

"Solid food is what I need." He headed for the crackers and cheese.

During the general shift toward the refreshments, Corinna followed Col. Smith. "Colonel, okay for me to use my bathroom?"

His mouth was full, but he nodded. She did intend to use her toilet and change clothes. But first she had to let Mr. Jacoby know that she'd be late to work.

No one was in the telephone room. She shut the door and placed her call to the office at the Gayety. The line was busy for quite a while, but finally Mr. Jacoby answered the phone. "Come as soon as you can," he said. "No double duty tonight. I hired a new girl today."

Corinna was about to leave when she heard voices in the hall. Nels Weigmann and Mr. Menafee were talking about the colonel and saying things she had no business to hear. She stood very still.

"Doug, you don't really know him the way I do. Take it from me, Smitty's a good buddy. He's just not a good loser if he's got a snoot-full."

"Maybe so, but from now on I'm not one of his poker pals. He just wants to win. He doesn't give two hoots for the strategy of the game."

"I've known Smitty ever since my first day at Walter Reed—before the sawbones took off his arm. We've played lots of cards. And split lots of bottles."

"You kept watching him. I was watching you. You're a sharp player, Nels."

"Thanks for the kind words. I thought he had the winning hand. The usual telltale signs—sweat and red streaks across his forehead."

"And he can't leave his hair alone."

"You've got him pegged. And you're going home the winner! I'm going home with my tail between my legs. I'll never tell Mid how much I lost tonight."

After that, everything got quiet. Corinna opened the door just a crack. No one was around. She ran to the colonel's living room. The lights were still on. Two quarters lay on the poker table. As usual, he'd locked the liquor cabinet before going to bed.

She grabbed the wastepaper basket and collected all the things needing a wash. She ran the leftovers to the icebox and pantry and the card table to the drawing room. It felt good to run. "Stop worrying," she told herself. "Tend to the poker table, and wash them ashtrays and dishes. Girl, everything gonna be all right."

13

After dinner, Nora and Flo went into the front hall to play jacks. They sat on the floor facing one another with legs widespread. Flo had hiked up her skirt, and the pale pink tulle surrounded her like a fancy ruffle. She had just bounced the ball for fivesies when the front door opened and Col. Smith appeared. The ball sped across the marble floor.

"I'll catch it!" Nora shouted. But the small brown ball, wedged under one of the claw feet of the table, was not easily found. By the time Nora got back, Flo was putting spit on a red place on her plump inner thigh.

"What happened?" Nora asked.

"He called me Toot-Toot-Tootsie." Flo unwrapped a Tootsie Roll.

"Col. Smith pinched your leg?"

Flo's mouth was full of candy. She nodded and handed the other half of the roll to Nora.

A door banged in the back hall. Mid called, "How about some lemonade? We're having it on the terrace."

"Daddy out there?"

"And Daddy Bill. Put the jacks away if you decide to join us." Mid hurried downstairs.

The adults were already sipping their drinks when the children arrived. Air as sultry as summertime held the sweet, rich aroma of Bill's cigar. The scent mingled with the fragrances of roses. Nels had landscaped the south side of the terrace with rose bushes. Quite a few were already in bloom.

"I saved these for you," Nels said. He gave the girls two boxes that had once held kitchen matches.

"Doodle bug houses!" Nora exclaimed.

The girls situated the houses in front of some red damask rose bushes. It was easy to find tenants.

"Doodle-doodle-doodle," Flo crooned. She watched the small, gray bugs roll into balls in her cupped hand.

"How many?" Nora asked.

"Three." Flo put them in her matchbox.

"I found five. I made a door for them. Now I'm going to build a fence."

Nora used dried twigs to enclose her matchbox

house. Flo looked under the nearest tree. Mature dogwoods shaded the long side of the terrace. Beneath the pink and white flowering trees were lots of sticks.

Mid delivered tumblers of lemonade to the girls, then seated herself in a rattan chair near her father. "How was Eddie today? Did he enjoy the strawberries?" she asked him.

"Maybe tomorrow. Today—well, he didn't have much of an appetite."

Nels had been inspecting the roses. He nipped off a long stemmed bud and smelled it. "I can't decide which ones are my favorites, the fragrant old-fashioned roses or the big hybrids." He gave the bud to Mid. "Eddie was in good spirits the last time I saw him. I'd taken him a cartoon, one of The Gumps, and it was just what the doctor ordered."

"Come to think of it," Bill said, "we had a good laugh this morning. We were playing our memory game, thinking back at least fifty years."

"What about?" Nels asked.

"Cap Dipple! Gosh, I'd just about forgotten him. Cap was a parrot. A big one from Panama."

"Was he green?" Nora asked.

"Mostly green, but he had yellow feathers on his head, and some red and blue in his tail. Cap could sing "I'm Forever Blowing Bubbles." If we gave him bites of apple, he'd sing it all the way through." Bill sang the chorus in a squawky parrot voice that made everybody laugh.

"Was he your parrot?" Flo asked. She went to sit near Bill's feet.

"No, he lived aboard a freighter. Eddie's father had a job at the Baltimore harbor. Once in a while, he'd take us there. Even when Cap wasn't in port, Eddie and I enjoyed looking around. All kinds of vessels, from all over the world. We got aboard one of them, a ship from the West Indies. Want to hear a scary story?"

"What scared you, Daddy Bill?" Nora sat down beside Flo.

Bill tossed the butt of his cigar into the rose bed. "They were taking on provisions. Crates of live chickens, sides of beef—all kinds of stuff. After that, the crew disappeared. Eddie and I were itching to go aboard. Nobody was around to stop us, so up the ladder we went! We'd just begun to look around when some guys spotted us. Of course, they bawled us out. Then they marched us to the hold. Do you know what's meant by a ship's hold?"

The girls shook their heads. Flo moved closer to Daddy Bill.

Bill took her on his lap. "It's where they store the cargo—whatever they're delivering. They opened a hatch in the deck so we could look down in the hold. They were hauling molasses."

"Tell us what scared you," Nora said. She was sharing her daddy's rattan settee.

"One of the men told us what had happened at sea. While the men were busy working, the cabin

boy decided to open the hatch. Apparently he bent way over to get a good look at the cargo. The ship lurched, and the kid fell into the molasses. He smothered to death."

"My God!" Nels exclaimed. "Why didn't somebody rescue him?"

"They didn't find him in time."

Nobody spoke. The only sounds were the calls of a pair of mourning doves. Flo whispered, "Please sing the song again. Like Cap Dipple?"

"AWK, AWK, SKEE-WAWK!" Bill sang and squawked. At the chorus, the children chimed in with extra squawks. They were both still singing and squawking as Mid escorted them into the house.

The terrace was dark. The only illumination came from the lights in the kitchen. Bill moved to a chair closer to the house. With his penknife he cut off the end of a long, thin cigar. While he smoked, he watched Nels stack chair cushions in the shelter created by the balcony. The job nearly done, he took his cushion to the pile. He cleared his throat.

"Something on your mind, Bill?"

Bill glanced up at the balcony, part of Letty Flagglar's suite. "Letty's out for the evening?"

"Dining in style at the Willard." Nels sat down on the rattan settee and used a chair as his hassock.

With a grin he said, "When she gets back, we'll know it. She'll turn on every light and wind up her victrola."

"Lois still complaining about the music?"

"Nope, Letty seems to have won that battle." Nels massaged the calf of his leg. "Something's bothering you. I wish you'd tell me about it."

Bill sat down beside him. "It's Eddie. And me. We can't take much more. I've about decided what to do, but..."

Despite the dim light, Nels could see the anguish in his face. "No matter what it is, you can tell me. I want to help."

Bill got up and stood in the shadows. When he spoke, his voice sounded muffled. "The cancer's spreading—getting its hooks in deep. Nothing kills the pain but morphine. You know that place. They're mighty free with food and prayers, but they don't hold with drugs. Eddie gets his morphine by the clock. Sometimes he's screaming, I'm going out of my mind, and the nurse says, 'We'll see to him, Mr. Norris. Why don't you go home for a while?'"

Nels went over and stood beside him. "Sometimes I dream that I'm in that hospital in Brest. Rows and rows of pallets, my buddies screaming and dying. "What a son of a bitch that doctor was! His answer to everything was amputation. Some of us got lucky. They shipped us home. Not that Walter Reed was any bed of roses. I was in and out of surgery for five years."

"How could you take it that long?"

"The damn leg's giving me fits." Nels motioned to the nearest chairs. As soon as they were seated, Nels said, "It seems crazy now—and God knows I was close to crazy then—but what got me through that nightmare was the German Luger in my kit."

"You'd use it—if you had to?"

"Not easy to put it into words—that pain. And desperation." He gave his leg a hard rub. "I dreaded surgery. And the future. No field engineering for me. Maybe no sweetheart. Forty years of poker and visiting the doctor. If those were the cards, I'd deal myself out of the game."

"What changed your mind?"

"The surgeon was a new guy, just out of Johns Hopkins. He offered me a choice, chronic osteomyelitis or amputation. I kept my leg and went back to school. A sassy little redhead seemed to like me."

Nels shifted in his chair so that he could face his father-in-law. "I'll never take the easy way out. How can I? Think of Mid. And Nora!"

He waited, hoping that Bill would say what had to be said. But there was only silence. "Smitty buttonholed me at dinner and tried to sell me his antique dueling pistols. He told me that you wanted his Colt revolver. Why, Bill?"

Bill's voice sounded tired, but firm. "Smitty's mistaken. I have no use for a gun."

The balcony light went on. Clear and sweet came the sound of recorded music—John McCormick singing "Roses of Picardy."

When the song ended, Bill stood up. "I need to get some sleep." He pressed Nels' shoulder.

"Rest well, Dad." Nels rose and followed him into the house.

JUNE

14

The eyes of the portrait seemed to be staring straight at her. Letty Flagglar sat up in bed and stared back. Narrow, gray-blue eyes smack up against a big, flat nose that veered to one side. At fourteen, her late husband had punched out his brother's front teeth. His brother had returned the favor by breaking Flag's nose. Nothing much had ever been done to fix the nose. The square-shaped face and big, square jaw were exactly like his. But the smile belonged to somebody else. Even in youth Flag had not had a generous, full-lipped mouth. Still, the artist had done a lovely job on the dress uniform. Size 44 long with three broad

gold stripes. Letty did not doubt that, wherever God had stationed him, Commander Josephus Flagglar was still wearing it.

Ten years ago, on the day of her husband's funeral, Letty had treated herself to an orgy of shopping. Among other things, she had selected a new frame for his portrait. In ornate gold leaf, it was the most costly frame that Harris & Ewing could provide.

"Flag, today's my birthday. Seventy! Want to see what you gave your little Boofies?"

She donned a new pink negligee and dyed-to-match mules. "See, Flag?" She added a diamond and platinum bar pin. "Who'd ever guess that you'd be so good to me!" Letty stood before the portrait and twirled. "Isn't this luscious? Mme. Gabrielle designed it. She does most of my clothes." Letty lifted her arms so her husband could appreciate the accordion-pleated sleeves. "Seven yards of material! They call this shade Ashes of Roses."

Somebody was tapping on the sitting room door.

Letty glanced at the bedside clock. A few minutes past seven. Who'd be calling at this hour? "Now, Flag, don't you go 'way. Boofies was awful naughty this year. I want you to hear all about it!" She hurried to open the door.

Janet Wilson smiled at her and presented a garment on a pink satin hanger. "Many happy returns of the day!"

"Why, what a nice way to start my birthday!"

The girl's smile broadened and revealed unusually pretty teeth. Letty thought, I must encourage her to smile more often. "Why are we standing in the hall? Step into my sittin' room, sugar!" Letty led the way.

"I can't stay but a minute. I have to eat and go to work."

Letty examined her gift. "Oh, it's my old dressing gown. I felt bad about putting it in the trash room, but the dear old thing was gettin' shabby." She ran her fingers over the new piping and lining. "You picked up the pink flowers in the pattern. Why, this garment is nicer than ever!" Letty gave Janet a kiss.

"You'll enjoy the lining. Slipper satin! Letty, I need to talk with you. Visit me this evening?"

"Count on me, sugar! I just have one other date today. Preston's treatin' me to lunch. My dear old beau never forgets his Letty."

"See you tonight!"

"Your place 'bout eight," Letty replied. Janet was worrying over something. Was Uncle Sam riffin' folks again? But why should the youngster mind losing that job? That typing pool was a waste of her time.

Tonight she'd hear the whole sorry tale and help if she could. But what she craved right now was a leisurely soak in jasmine-scented water. On the way to the bathroom, she stuck out her tongue at the Commander.

KALORAMA

The texture of the huge, pink towel felt like velvet. Letty smiled as she examined herself. Plump but healthy. "Meilleurs felicitations, Letitia Hopkins Flagglar!" She slipped into the robe that Janet had renewed for her.

At eight, Corinna arrived with the breakfast tray. Flo was with her. "Happy birthday to you!" they sang. The child's performance, without giggles, showed that they had been practicing.

Letty thanked them. "Corinna, I'll have my breakfast on the balcony. The roses are glorious this morning."

"This gonna be a fine day. Miz Flagglar, there's a little something from me on the tray."

Letty picked up a tumbler filled with pink roses. "Oh, Corinna, they smell so sweet!" She held the glass so Florence could enjoy the fragrance. "June is the month of roses. My mother wanted to name me Rose. Wouldn't that have been the ideal name for me? Daddy named me Letitia Belle after his paternal grandmother."

Florence was looking at the bran muffins. She followed Corinna through the French doors that led to the balcony. Letty gestured for the child to sit at the table. Corinna handed Flo a glass of milk and poured Mrs. Flaggar's first cup of coffee.

"Everything like you wants it, Miz Flagglar?" Corinna asked.

Letty was spreading butter on Flo's hot muffin. "Everything's fine, Corinna. How did you know to bring enough for two?"

"A little bird told me you was having company." Corinna laid the platter of scrambled eggs and bacon on the wrought iron table.

After the click of the sitting room door, Letty and Flo gave their full attention to the food. The only sounds were birdcalls and the occasional scraping of a spoon, Flo helping herself to peach preserves.

At the end of the meal, Letty tilted her face and stretched her arms toward the sun. "How lovely!"

"Mimi likes it out here, too. May I get her?" Flo asked.

Letty nodded. Mimi was the long-legged French doll that sat on Letty's bed.

As soon as Flo and Mimi were settled, Letty said, "I don't let most children play with Mimi. You're special. Nora is, too. Both of you are gentle with her."

Flo was carefully examining Mimi's many petticoats. All were pink, but differed in fabric and hue. "Mrs. Flagglar, why do you like pink so much?"

Letty thought a while before she answered. She believed in honesty, especially when talking with children. "I got married on my eighteenth birthday. My husband hated pink. In fact, the only

color he would buy was blue. For fifty-two years I lived with navy blue, sky blue, aquamarine, and every other kind of blue there is. All the while I was longin' for pink."

"That's why you put pink wallpaper in all your rooms."

"It looks like wallpaper, but it's what they call 'watered silk'. I had to send away for it. It came all the way from France. I couldn't find the right color anywhere else. You see, I wanted it like my face powder."

The child looked puzzled.

Letty led the way to the loveseat in her sitting room. "You and Mimi wait for me, you hear? I'll show you what I mean." She didn't want a little explorer to discover her dressing room. Too many valuables would be put at risk. Too many reasons for saying no. She hated having to say no to Florence.

Moments later, Flo was looking into a cut-crystal box filled with face powder.

"Come over here, sugar," Letty said. "Now take a good look. Does my powder match the silk on the wall?" She held the box against the wall and low enough so Florence could easily compare the two.

"They're alike!" Flo exclaimed.

"Exactly the same shade?"

"Zactly." Looking around the large sitting room, Flo pointed to the portrait above the fireplace.

"Jody," she said. On the mantel stood dozens of smaller pictures in silver frames. All showed the same person, as man or boy. "I remember what you told me. He got sick and died. On the boat coming home from the war."

"Jody died of influenza. But I must not dwell on that. My son left me lots of happy things to think about."

They were looking through a photograph album when a loud rapping startled them. Flo ran to open the door.

Lois Haskell glared at her child. "I told you to go downstairs and wait for me, Florence. I've spent the past half-hour trying to find you!"

"She came to wish me a happy birthday. Forgive me for keepin' her so long." Letty was glad to see the look of fear leave the child's face.

Lois put her arms around Letty and kissed her on the cheek. "Why, of course I do. Congratulations!"

"Lois, honey, you're too slim. Are you gettin' enough to eat?"

"Applesauce! Who wants to be fat? Come on, Florence. Let's see if the dining room's still open. It better be, or you'll be in trouble."

Letty watched as the Haskells sped down the stairs. Lois seemed friendly, but probably they'd never be more than good neighbors. With Flo it could be different.

"I simply dote on that child!" Letty told herself.

Letty glanced at the grandfather clock in the lobby of the Kennedy-Warren. Just past noon. Seated in his usual armchair, Preston Emory was reading the latest issue of *Liberty*. Letty recognized the caricature of FDR on the cover of the magazine.

Feeling entirely at home, she took a familiar route through the maze of fading American oriental rugs, highly polished furniture, and slipcovered sofas and chairs. Preston's apartment-hotel reminded her of many other places she had known.

She tiptoed behind his chair and covered his eyes with her small, gloved hands. She kissed the top of his freshly barbered white hair. "Guess who, precious!"

At once, he stood and embraced her. "Sweetheart, you look like a million bucks. Happy birthday!" He presented a corsage of camellias, which he pinned to the lapel of her white linen suit.

"How come you always know exactly what I want?" The flowers matched the deep pink of her satin blouse, kid pumps and purse.

"How come you always smell so good?" He tucked her arm under his. "The feast awaits us. Let's eat!"

As they entered the dining room, Letty noticed that they were attracting attention. She and Preston looked nice together. At seventy and seventy-two, both of them looked a lot younger, she thought. He was six inches taller than she and not one bit fat. Preston had an excellent tailor.

Out of uniform, Flag had always looked tacky. He'd been just plain pigheaded when it came to spending money on civvies. One Christmas he'd refused to accept her gift. He'd been real ugly about it—demanding to see the bill and ordering her to return the dinner jacket.

Preston never acted ugly. Different from Flag in every conceivable way. Truly the only thing her men had in common was herself.

She took her first sip of white wine. "Can I guess the menu?"

"Chicken à la reine soup, salade vinaigrette, sole almandine. With fresh parsley." He winked at her.

"One French pastry or two?"

"One here, one for later."

She blew a kiss across the table. As usual, Preston had arranged for all the things she liked best.

"Don't I see a new piece of jewelry?" He indicated the diamond pin on her blouse.

"Flag gave it to me. Like it?"

"The Commander's taste seems to be improving. At his current rate of expenditure, he'll

exhaust his resources in about thirty years." Preston was an investment banker and had been the Flagglars' financial advisor.

"Thirty? On my last birthday, you said fifty."

He chuckled. "Don't worry about it, Letty. If you ever do spend all the Flagglar money, you can share mine."

After the wine and so much loving, Letty felt sleepy. She whispered, "I need to snuggle against your big back."

Obligingly, Preston turned on his side . "Letty, when are you going to marry me?"

She felt too sleepy to embroider the truth. "I love you to death, I always have, but I don't want to get married. I've told you so a million times."

"You think that marriage would change me. I'd be like Joe Flaggler."

She put a row of soft kisses across his back.

"Don't I make you happy, Letty?"

"Yes, you do." She tightened her embrace.

"One afternoon, years ago, I wandered into a flower garden. A beautiful young woman was holding her baby and sobbing. I lent her a handkerchief. And gave her my heart. Dearest, I want to take care of you."

He turned over and looked at her. "You stayed with him for fear of losing your child. I understand

that. But why would you marry that bastard when you won't marry me?"

"Must you know everything about me?"

"Tell me that much, Letty."

After a pause she said, "I was seventeen when Momma got sick. Daddy brought me home from school. I loved Momma, and I was glad to do for her. But nursin' is a hard job. I was runnin' up and down those stairs all day long. Towards the last, I slept beside her. I was holding her the night she passed away. Everything changed after that. It got so bad that I was praying to God to take me too.

"Daddy was always goin' off, never tellin' where or why. He put me in charge of that great big old place. I tried—truly I tried—but nothin' I did pleased Daddy. Sometimes he'd punish me. I try not to remember how mean he could be." Despite her resolve to forget, she remembered clearly the sting of her father's leather belt. "I had to get away from him. When Flag proposed, I said yes."

Preston took her into his arms. "You had to get away from your father, and Joe came along at the right time. But what's any of that got to do with not marrying me?"

"There's something wrong with me—something that makes men enjoy hurting me. Oh, not at first! For a long time I thought Flag loved me. He'd be moody sometimes because he wanted a son. It seemed like I couldn't give him any babies. Finally I got pregnant, but instead of being loving

to me, Flag was mean. After Jody came, all Flag truly enjoyed was inventing new ways to make me grovel." He'd expected the boy to be an unspoiled version of himself. Instead, Jody took after the Hopkins, handsome of face and average of stature. She'd managed to keep him at a respectful distance from his father. Their relationship was cordial, but never close.

"I would never hurt you, Letty. Never." Preston kissed the palms of her hands. When she didn't speak, he turned on his side. She pressed her body against his. As he had done many times over the years, he lay very still and hummed them both to sleep.

It was just past eight o'clock when Letty entered the smallest bedroom on Third Floor.

"Janet, you've turned this room into a real cozy home. Lots of changes since the last time I was here."

"Partly thanks to you, Letty. See how you've helped me?" Janet indicated the armchair where Letty was about to sit.

Letty took a careful look at it. "You used the tapestry I put in the trash room. Flag got it at a bazaar in Burma. Why I hung on to that old blue bedspread is somethin' I don't know."

"You were saving it for me! I'm so glad we use the same trash room."

KALORAMA

Letty was inspecting the job of reupholstery. "Sugar, this is lovely work. The folks at Biggs should take a few lessons from you."

Janet opened her wardrobe closet and took out a child's tweed coat, leggings, and bonnet. She handed them to Letty. "What do you think?"

Letty took several minutes to examine the garments. "I'm impressed. Of course, I knew you could sew. But this smocking and tailoring—why, Mme. Gabrielle couldn't do a better job. Who taught you to sew like this?"

"Mom was a seamstress. Mostly she worked at home. I've been sewing all my life. Do you really like Antoinette's fall outfit?"

"I like it a whole lot, but who is Antoinette?"

"My daughter."

"I didn't know you had a child. How old is she?"

"Three next October." Janet indicated a framed photograph. It stood on a small desk near Letty's chair. "That's my daughter."

It was the picture of a pretty child with lots of light brown ringlets. A mulatto child. "You married a colored man?" Letty asked in surprise.

"I fell in love with Tony. But Antoinette is all that's left of our years together. Letty, I don't even have a ring. Nothing at all to show her."

Janet told the story of how they had met at the Chastleton. Janet worked in the office of the hotel. Tony played the Steinway grand piano on the mezzanine.

KALORAMA

"Tony knows how to read music, but mostly he plays by ear," Janet said. "Any piece the guests wanted to hear, Tony could play—popular songs, big band music, jazz. Oh, he's a fine musician." Janet's eyes filled with tears. "For a while he thought he loved me."

"You've separated, but he supports the child?"

"Not any more. No one helps. My father won't have anything to do with me. Or his grandchild. She's been living with Tony's married sister, but now they're moving away. I haven't been able to find another place for her. Nothing safe."

"I don't see why you waited so long to tell me all this. Were you afraid I couldn't understand?"

"Oh, what am I going to do?" Janet covered her face with her hands.

"Where are these people going?"

"Texas. They go on the first day of July. They'll be living with friends. And there's no room for Antoinette. Anyhow, I couldn't bear for us to live so far apart."

Letty reached for the photograph. "If Antoinette were my child, what on earth would I do?" She sighed. "Nothin' comes to mind. But don't you worry. I'll put on my thinkin' cap." She gave Janet a kiss. "See you tomorrow night, sugar."

KALORAMA

It was close to midnight. Lefty pulled the gold and jade chain of her bedside lamp. The carved jade base was about a thousand years old. "You belong in the Smithsonian Museum," she told it. For nearly two hours she'd been lying in the dark, planning Antoinette's future.

She opened the top drawer of her dresser. The Commander seemed to be watching as she removed a heavy gold band from a small velvet box.

"Remember, Flag? Fifty-two years ago today. I'm glad it's not engraved. I'm goin' to get it done at Galts. "For Janet from Tony." Something for the child to see.

Letty left the ring in the center of the dresser scarf and got back into bed. "Bringin' up a child the right way is a big responsibility," she said. The Commander did not appear to disagree. "I did a real fine job of raising Jody. You said so yourself. Mostly I worked hard at finding the right schools and camps. It took a lot of snooping, but sometimes I saved him from a real bad choice. That military school you went to would have been terrible for a sensitive boy like Jody.

"But I can't save Antoinette that way. Colored people don't get treated right in the States.

"You know what, Flag? I'm thinking of going into business—investing in a fancy shop in Paris. Janet can be my representative and make baby clothes. Truly it won't matter what she sews, just so it's lovely and she enjoys doin' it.

"Gabrielle will help me. I know she will. Before she married her American soldier, she had a boutique in Rue St. Anne. That's where we met. I'll make it worth her while to find me a small business. One that needs a partner with plenty of money."

Preston would help with the rest. He knew everything about making business deals. And he'd do it in no time! His smart, fast moves had saved her from losing all her money in '29. But he didn't really know Paris. What fun to introduce him to her favorite spots! She closed her eyes and imagined being in Paris with Preston. An evening in mid-July, les illuminations, la Rive Gauche.

She got up and unhooked the portrait from the wall. "No more hard feelings. No feelings of any kind. Flag, you're heading for dry dock, but I'm heading into exciting new waters. If Janet's willing, we'll go full steam ahead!"

She carried the portrait into the dark hall closet and left the Commander, face down, on the floor.

Settling between her satin sheets, she whispered, "Miss Letty, don't you forget to rescue the frame!" What did she want instead of the portrait? She fell asleep picturing a still life of roses, buds to full-blown. Mostly pinks.

15

The front door lights were still on. Janet put down the suitcase and shifted the sleeping child. Her key was almost in the lock when the door swung open.

Corinna gave the signal for no talking. "She be sound asleep. Ain't we lucky!" she whispered.

"Antoinette was too excited to sleep on the train. Why are we whispering?"

"The Weigmanns been fussin' again. Ain't smart to wake 'em up. " Corinna locked the front door and turned off some lights. Suitcase in hand, she began climbing the stairs to Janet's room.

With both arms around Antoinette, Janet followed. By the time she stepped into the room, Corinna had already removed the bedspread and turned back the top sheet. Together they took off

the child's sandals and dress. While they were tucking her in, Antoinette opened her eyes and smiled.

Janet closed each eye with a gentle kiss. "Go back to sleep, honey. It's way past your bedtime."

"She gots your smile. Blue eyes, too. And her daddy give her a real pretty suntan. Just like mine." Corinna's dimple appeared.

"At the farm I spent lots of time in the sunshine. I was hoping for a nice tan, but all I got was pink."

Corinna studied Janet's complexion. "You needs cocoa butter. Rub it on real good."

"Letty gave me a bar just before I went to Manassas. How is she? Everything set for tomorrow?"

"Breakfast in her suite at eight sharp. Real fancy breakfast for four. Why do she want it for four?"

"Mr. Emory is going with us. Letty says he'll fix everything. He's got connections. Corinna, it's really true, isn't it? Antoinette and I are going to live together. In Paris!"

"It sure do look that way. Girl, I gots to get to my night job. You be needing me tomorrow?"

Janet thought for a moment. "Post a letter for me?"

"Just you leaves it on the bureau." Corinna took another look at Antoinette. "See you in the morning!"

Janet set about the task of writing to her father. It was the last thing she had to do before getting some much needed rest. On the desk were her fountain pen, stamps, and stationery. But she couldn't keep her mind on the letter. Instead, she thought about her busy weekend at the farm.

Antoinette's clothes had taken most of her time—so many things to wash, hang on the line, iron, and pack. And she'd made a good many efforts to express her thanks. Somehow or other, the right words never really got said. How could she adequately thank Tony's sister? For over a year Antoinette had been treated like the baby of the family. Her aunt, uncle, and cousins had welcomed her with open arms. And they'd all gone along to the train station to wave goodbye. Usually the night train to Washington came and went without excitement. This time the platform rang with the sound of young voices as hugs and kisses were exchanged and Janet handed out her gifts of candy bars. To her relief, no one had cried.

Janet crumpled the sheet of stationery and reached for a small bundle of old letters in the desk drawer. She had sent them to her father. Each letter had been promptly returned, apparently unread. She didn't know why she had kept them, but she was glad she had. They might get her ready to write again. After checking the postmarks, she opened the oldest one.

January 6, 1934

Dear Father,

I feel confused and in terrible pain. Somehow I must get word to you. You don't answer the telephone.

Ruth called me. At services this morning, Pastor Kauffman announced that Mom had passed away on December 30. He said that she had been in Norfolk General and died during surgery. Ruth found out that she was buried in Baltimore. Loudon Cemetery, beside Aunt Frieda. Father, is this true?

Ruth went to the house, but you weren't home. The neighbors expect you back tonight. I'll try to get you on the phone.

WHY DIDN'T YOU TELL ME?
PLEASE CALL ME RIGHT AWAY.

Your loving daughter,
Janet

January 12, 1934

Dear Father,

My letter came back today. You hung up the phone as soon as you heard my voice. I called Ruth, and she said that you hang up on her, too.

KALORAMA

Every night I dream that I see Mom. I try to reach her, but something gets in the way. I search and search for her until I wake up crying.

Last night the dream seemed so real. Mom and I were hemming gowns for a wedding. Nine bridesmaids and a matron of honor, and every dress was size sixteen or larger. Sixty yards of taffeta. We were talking about Helen Trent. That girl was like a close friend, not just a voice on the radio. Mom couldn't decide what Helen ought to do.

Father, I need to know about Mom. When did she get sick? Did she ask for me? Did she leave me a message?

Please call me right away.

Janet

January 20, 1934

Dear Father,

Antoinette and I were at your door. We needed you. How could you lock us out? How could you stand to hear us knocking and crying? Antoinette cried until she finally fell asleep on the train.

What am I to do? You return my letters. You hang up when I get you on the phone. You

refuse to talk to Pastor Kauffman. He wants to help, but you won't let him.

So much has happened that I hardly know where to start. About a year ago, Tony got a job with a dance band. They're on the road all the time. He used to come home when he could, and he sent me money. Not anymore. His sister found out that Tony married the girl who sings with the band. When I heard about it, I thought the pain would kill me. It didn't. Only my pride hurts now.

At last I've landed a full-time job in a typing pool at the General Accounting Office. Antoinette will be living in Manassas with Tony's married sister. They are good people, but I am praying very hard that my baby and I can soon live together again.

We need you, Father, and you need us. PLEASE CALL.

Janet

April 14, 1934

Dear Father,

Both of us have had the grippe, but we're okay now. I see Antoinette every weekend. She's so much prettier than I was as a child.

KALORAMA

Her hair is taffy colored, and her skin is like coffee with lots of cream in it. Her eyes are even bluer than Mom's. Unless she's asleep, she's on the go. She's starting to get a mind of her own, a bright one.

As always, I will write my telephone number and address on the back of the envelope. Please note the changes: Emerson 5-0579, 1867 Kalorama Road, N.W.

My boss at General Accounting has taken me under her wing. Her name is Roberta McElroy. I now live in the boardinghouse where she lives. My room is small, but I get two big meals every day.

Father, I keep praying that you will forgive me.

Your loving daughter,
Janet

Janet tore the old letters and envelopes into small scraps and dropped them into the wastebasket. Her new message would be short—hardly more than a note. After that, she'd be able to sleep. Or was she forgetting something? She glanced around the room. The outfits for tomorrow were ready. There was only one other thing she intended to do.

KALORAMA

In her purse was a small, black velvet box containing a heavy gold wedding band. Engraved inside it were the words that Letty had chosen.

FOR JANET WITH ALL MY LOVE, TONY

She slipped the ring on the fourth finger of her left hand before beginning the letter to her father.

June 30, 1935

Dear Father,

By the time you receive this letter, we'll be on the Queen Mary. Antoinette and I are going to live in France.

My best friend is Letty Flagglar. She's going to buy a partnership in a fancy shop in Paris. I'll be her representative as well as a designer and seamstress.

Letty knows Paris, and she'll help us get settled. She plans to visit us, but most of the time, she'll be at Kalorama, 1867 Kalorama Road, N.W.

Antoinette is pretty, and she is very bright. She sings or talks most of the time. There is no reason for you to feel anything but proud of your only grandchild.

We'll send you a postcard from Paris.

God be with you, Father,
Janet

She put a three cent stamp on the envelope and wrote her father's address. It had been more than a year since her last letter to him. Would he read this one? She hoped so, but she no longer feared a future without him. So many wonderful things were happening. Miraculous things. Maybe Mom was looking out for them.

Always before, Janet had recorded her address on the back of the envelope. This time she also put it on the front. In the upper left hand corner she carefully printed

**J. & A. WILSON
PARIS, FRANCE**

JULY

16

When Nora got back from the movie matinee, she went upstairs to find Flo.

"She slipped out while I was taking my nap," Lois Haskell said. "She hasn't finished packing. We leave tomorrow or we'll miss the July 4 celebrations. Find her for me, Nora?"

Everything about Flo's mother looked too blonde. Even her blue eyes seemed pale. "Sure, Mrs. Haskell. I'll get her right away."

Nora knew about the Haskells' vacation. A long time ago, Daddy had mentioned it. Now Flo talked about it all the time. Her Uncle Earl had a

big house near the ocean. Flo would be going to the beach every day.

Nora also knew that nobody else was at home on Second Floor. Mrs. Flagglar was in Paris, and the Menafees had gone to Baltimore for the day. On the third floor she knocked, then banged on every door. No answer. Outside Miss Esther's room, she sat on the carpet to rest and think. Who might know where Flo was?

She found Corinna in the drawing room. "Where's Flo?" she asked.

"I ain't seen her since you gone to the movies. That child carried on something terrible. Flo sure be wanting to see that show." Corinna set up a card table.

"The serial ended today, and it was swell! Maybe she's in the kitchen?"

"Ain't nobody down there. Mr. Norris gone to the hospital with a real fancy lunch for his friend. Your momma and daddy gone shopping. Now you leave me be. I got my work to do." She straightened the legs of another card table.

"Flo must be outside. I'll skate around the block."

Her skates were not in the umbrella stand or anywhere else in the telephone room. Flo must have borrowed them. Boy, oh boy, she'd be in trouble if her mother found out! Mrs. Haskell would never forgive ugly knees.

Flo wasn't on the front porch or the terrace. Nobody was skating down Kalorama Road.

KALORAMA

"Where is Florence Haskell?" Nora asked everybody she saw.

"She was in my yard looking for Pixie," Mr. Ayres' narrow, bony face looked angry. "Damn mutt disappeared months ago." He acted like he was too busy to talk.

Nora didn't know what to do. She went home and sat at the top of the front steps.

"What's up, Snooks?" Bobbie McElroy climbed up and sat beside her. She put several packages near her feet on the step below.

"Flo's not in the house. She's not outside. I can't find her!" With Aunt Bobbie's arms around her, Nora couldn't hold back her tears.

When the crying stopped, Bobbie found a handkerchief for her. "Somehow or other, you've managed to miss one another. Don't worry. We'll find her. But first, let's stop by my room. I have to unload these shoes. Nora, I got three pairs half-soled for fifty cents!" She collected her bundles. "I'll fix us something cool to drink."

It wasn't long before Nora was washing her hands and face with Cashmere Bouquet soap. After that, Bobbie handed her a glass of lemonade. Nora sat down on the steamer trunk to drink it.

Bobbie carried her glass to the table beside her easy chair. As soon as she sat down, she lit a cigarette. "While you were freshening up, I saw Lois. She looks terrible—thinks she's caught the grippe. And she hasn't seen Florence." Bobbie

took several swallows of lemonade. "Where can that child be? As soon as we finish our drinks, you'll check Fourth Floor. I'll do the cellar."

"Aunt Bobbie, I'm not allowed on Fourth."

"Are you allowed in the cellar?"

"Yes, but..." Nora didn't know how to finish the sentence. The cellar was where Daddy tended the furnace. One morning while they were down there, a big load of coal got delivered. Soot landed everywhere. Even the insides of their noses got black. Lumps of coal clattered down a metal chute. The racket went on and on until the coal bin couldn't hold any more. The cellar was a dark, spooky place. Sometimes Corinna had to set traps. "I'd rather not go down there alone."

"Okay, I'll do the cellar. You have my permission to check Fourth." Bobbie led the way to the stairs. "This is like hide-and-seek. I'm betting on you to win!" She was smiling as she started down. Nora hurried up.

Fourth Floor had pale yellow walls and brown doors, much like Third. The ceiling was lower, and the windows were smaller. Everything else seemed familiar, especially the way it smelled. Corinna always sprinkled O'Cedar on her mop before dusting the floors. This hall had no carpet. A swell place to skate, Nora decided.

Seven doors. One was Corinna's. The others belonged to the college men. Nora knocked and called, but no one came. At one end of the hall, in

partial view, was a big lavatory. At the other end was the only other door left to try. Nora banged, called, then twisted the knob. The open doorway revealed a flight of stairs. Where to? She had no idea. Stepping between pails, mops, and brooms, she started down, the only way she could go.

Lucky she'd left the door open! Nine steps curved down to a landing. The next flight looked straighter and longer. Beyond it? It was too dark down there to tell. Without a railing to hang onto, she moved slowly and kept one hand on the wall.

The farther down she climbed, the darker it got. She was in almost total darkness when she stepped on something that rolled farther down the stairs. With a loud gasp, she slid along the bricks of the outer wall. As she steadied herself, she heard the skate bumping and rolling to a stop far below. Nora felt around and found her other skate. Its strap was missing.

"Flo!" she called. "I know you're down there! Have you got my strap?"

Flo didn't answer.

Nora felt sweaty and itchy, and her left eye was stinging. When she touched her face, her fingers made little balls of dirt. With the bottom of her skirt she wiped her face until it was fairly dry.

It was too dark to see a path. Old newspapers and lots of magazines had been stacked against the walls, and some had slipped. She was moving slowly when both of her feet flew out from under

her. Unhurt but breathless, she landed at the bottom of the flight. Bundles fell past her and bumped into other things below. As the stacks collapsed, light appeared.

A small oval window was just above the landing. And there her skate was on the next step! After a bout of sneezing she claimed it. Through spider webs and dirty window glass, she looked down at the side lawn and driveway. With a tight grip on both skates, she began the last flight. Her skinned knees hurt and were bleeding.

Bags of empty bottles and bundles of old clothes lined the walls, but she moved as fast as she could toward the last landing. And a door! She pulled it toward her and saw, just beyond, some heavy blue draperies. She was about to push through them and yell "I win!" when she heard a woman's voice.

Through a narrow gap where the portieres came together, she saw Col. Smith's back hall. He was there! Corinna was there, too, holding a scrub brush in one hand and a pair of rompers in the other. Whatever she'd said had made the colonel very mad. He snatched the rompers and slapped her hard across the face. Corinna staggered, but she didn't fall down or cry.

"Keep your mouth shut," he said. "This has nothing to do with you."

Corinna's bottom lip was bleeding and making spots on her uniform. She was heading for the portieres.

Nora stepped behind the door and put both hands over her mouth. Her heart was making such big thumps that her whole chest hurt. Could they hear the thumps?

Corinna pushed through the drapes and went up the stairs. She was crying and never looked back.

Where was the colonel? Nora listened, and in a little while she heard water running in his bathroom. As fast as she could, she ran through his rooms to the safety of her parents' suite.

"So there you are!" Mid exclaimed. She fastened the belt of her green taffeta dinner skirt and began to button the front of a white organdy blouse. "First we couldn't find Flo. Then we couldn't find you! Now it looks as though the two of you have been playing in the cellar. Is that the story?" She was frowning, and her voice had a sharp edge that told Nora she was in serious trouble.

"No, M'am, I wasn't in the cellar. I don't know where Flo is." The look of angry disbelief on her mother's face kept her from saying more. She wanted to tell where she had been and what she'd overheard, but this was not the time to do it. Momma would call her a snooper and spank her with the hairbrush. Momma hated kids with big ears.

Mid sprinkled cologne on her handkerchief and slipped it into the seam pocket of her skirt. "Flo will show up when she gets hungry. Lois is ill…just

wants soup and tea. Corinna's willing to take up the tray, but says she's ill, too—too ill to wash dishes. Oh, why does everything go wrong on bridge night?"

Mid watched as Nels selected a tie to wear with his gray suit. "That old red one? Why don't you wear the green paisley? And why are you smiling, Nels? I see nothing amusing about any of this."

Nels winked at Nora. "Sure am glad to see you, Miss Eleanora! I couldn't find you. We were beginning to worry."

Mid took off Nora's dress. "My word! Just look at this thing! Why, I could plant petunias on it. How did you manage to get so dirty?"

Nora opened her mouth to answer, but Mid cut her off. "I'll hear about it later. And it better be good! Nels, see that she takes a bath. With soap. But make it fast! No duets. In twenty minutes the food's got to be on the sideboard."

"What are we having?" Nora asked.

"Ham, baked beans, raw vegetable tray with spring onions, and hot rolls."

"What's for dessert?"

"Fruit compote and raspberry jelly roll. Oh, and we're having some of Pop's watermelon pickles." Mid took off Nora's socks and shoes. "You'd better not dawdle, or the pickles will be gone."

"Can you save me some? Please, Momma?"

Mid opened the door. "I'll think about it."

KALORAMA

"What would you say to a soapy suit?" Nels threw a generous handful of lavender-scented salts into the bath water.

Nora stepped into the tub. "Only little kids get soapy suits."

Nels rolled up his sleeves. "Is that so? Well, I'm sorry to hear it. A soapy suit is the best way to get nice and clean. And to look for athlete's foot." He knelt on the bathmat and picked up Nora's right foot.

"Daddy, I have an awful lot to tell you. Some scary parts, too."

Nels examined Nora's left foot. "After dinner we'll talk. Just you, your mother, and I. I want to hear it, but we're short on time. Not now. The three of us can handle anything. Even the scary parts."

Nora closed her eyes and waited while she got her soapy stockings. Oh, please, she prayed, don't let me have athlete's foot! She could almost feel the swab and smell Daddy's Magic Mix that burned like fire. Worst of all, he always reminded her that "when he was a little girl, he never cried. Plucky kids don't cry over little hurts."

"Healthy pigs!" Nels declared. He rubbed the bar of Lux on the washrag, then made long gloves for her fingers and arms.

"Daddy, do you remember Forty Knocker?"

"You bet!"

"Will you do it?"

"Sure, but weren't you complaining about baby stuff?"

"Please?"

"I'll do the washing. You recite the words, but not too fast."

Nels got the cloth ready to wash Nora's face. "Ready...get set...go!"

"Forty knocker

Eye-ee winker

Nosey smeller

Mouth-ee eater

Chin-ee chopper!"

Just in time, Nels dodged the water. He used the bathmat to soak it up.

"I want to do the rest by myself," Nora said.

He handed her the long-handled brush. "Don't forget your back. Get dressed, and wait for me. If you're gorgeous, I just might escort you to dinner."

"Can I wear what I want?"

"Not this time. Your mother laid it out on your bed."

"Save me some watermelon pickles?"

"Nora, you know very well that she's already done that. Okay, I'll add a few more." He took his jacket off the door hook.

"I've got to tell you something, Daddy. Please stay."

"I've already stayed too long, Nora. I'm needed downstairs. After dinner we'll have lots of time to talk." He kissed the top of her head.

It was exactly six o'clock when Nels started back for Nora. The Menafees were heading down to the dining hall. He greeted them in mid-stairs.

"I was afraid we'd miss dinner," Edith said. "I think every vehicle in Baltimore is going somewhere tonight."

"Thirty-five minutes just to get out of the city," Doug said. "Say, is Bill downstairs? I bought a book today that's bound to interest him."

"He'll be joining us for bridge. He's spent most of the day with Eddie."

Smitty barely nodded as he pushed past them. He looked flushed and untidy and in a great hurry to get to dinner. The scent of bourbon lingered after him.

"That man needs a cup of strong coffee," Nels said.

In the entrance hall Nels met Bobbie, Walt, and Esther, all inquiring about Flo.

"Nobody knows where she went," Nels said.

"About two o'clock she came to see me," Esther said. "Not much of a visit. Walt and I were leaving." She smiled at Walt. "Our class at Arthur Murray's."

Walt smiled back. "Esther gave her a bag of snacks."

"The little thing seemed hungry."

Bobbie let out a deep breath. "Oh, God, please let her show up soon!"

"If she's not here by seven, I'll call the police," Nels said. "Lois won't let me do it until then. She thinks that Flo will want her dinner and come home."

"Daddy!" Nora ran across the hall. "Why didn't you come for me?"

With a dramatic flourish, Nels offered Nora his arm, and they led the way to the stairs. "Wait a minute, folks!" Nels told the others. "Corinna's bringing a heavy tray. Steady there, Corinna. Take your time."

"What's wrong with her, Nels?" Bobbie spoke in a penetrating whisper. "Has she been drinking?"

"The colonel hit her!" Nora said. "He told her not to tell."

Corinna began to shudder from head to toe. Nels made a grab for the tray, but he was too late. China, glass, and liquids landed on the marble floor. Nels and Walt quickly piled the fragments on the tray.

"Corinna, do you know where Flo went?" Bobbie asked.

Corinna seemed dazed, unaware that she was standing in a puddle of soup.

Esther pulled her out of the wet. "What do you know about the child?"

Corinna did not answer. Like the others she was watching Nels. He'd carried the tray to the dumbwaiter. He glanced inside, set the tray on the floor, and reached far into the dumbwaiter. His body blocked the view, as he opened one door, closed it, and set the tray on the floor. It was when he backed out that everyone got a glimpse of Flo's blonde hair and bare shoulders.

"The colonel...?" Corinna fell to her knees on the wet floor.

Nora ran toward the dumbwaiter. "Flo's got to wake up. And get dressed for dinner."

Nels stopped her. He handed the tray to Walt. "Tell Mid that Corinna had an accident. Nothing else, understand?"

"What about Smitty?"

"He's in the dining hall. Keep him talking and telling jokes. The authorities will be here soon. Can you do it, Walt?"

"I can try. Come with me, Esther?"

"Bobbie, take care of Nora," Nels said. Keep her in her room."

"But why must I go to my room? Why don't you make Flo get out of there?" Nora burst into tears.

Nels carried her into her bedroom. "Nora, you're not being punished. You and Bobbie are helping me. Pretty soon we'll have our dinner." With a nod to Bobbie he closed the door.

It took only a few minutes to notify the police. As Nels left the telephone room, he saw that Corinna was trying to go upstairs. "I can't walk good," she said.

"I'll help you." Nels steadied himself against the railing and kept one arm around Corinna. Slowly they made their way to her room on Fourth Floor. Nels took off her shoes and helped her get into bed. "What makes you suspect Col. Smith?" he asked.

"I was scrubbing the bathroom floor and found a pair of rompers under the tub. That's all I know."

"Corinna, you're running a fever. The best thing for you to do now is put it out of your mind."

With a weary sigh she rolled on her side and closed her eyes. Nels did not leave her until he was sure she was asleep.

Mid was in the entrance hall. "I took Lois her supper, and I mopped up the mess on this floor." She stared at the tears running down his face. "Nels, what's wrong?"

Nels opened his arms, and Mid moved into them. "You found Flo?" she whispered.

"A little while ago. She's dead. I'll tell you what I know, but let's sit in the drawing room. I've got to rest my leg."

He chose the sofa that faced Kalorama Road and seated her beside a colorful arrangement of zinnias. Mid had cut them before breakfast. This morning? It felt like years ago.

Mid looked at the flowers, then at him. "Why are you stalling? How bad is it?"

"I don't know the best way to tell you." He took hold of her hand.

"Where is Flo now?"

"Where we found her, sitting way back in the dumbwaiter. No pulse. No heartbeat. Nora thinks that Flo was hiding and fell asleep."

"Nora saw her!"

"Quite a few saw her—Bobbie, Esther, Walt, and Corinna. Corinna suspects Smitty. So do I."

"Smitty? Oh, no!"

A vehicle with flashing lights paused in front of Kalorama, and two men in uniform got out. Nels went to let them in.

17

The days that followed weighed heavily on Nels. He dealt with visiting authorities and unhappy tenants, did what he could for his deeply depressed wife, and protected Nora from learning the truth.

It was mid-morning before Nels could start to repair the kitchen light. The big room was fragrant with the spicy scent of fresh-baked gingerbread. At work atop a tall ladder, Nels felt anything but cool. By the time he'd located the short, sweat was stinging his eyes. He decided to treat himself to a break before finishing the job.

He drank a large glass of water, inserted a rubber stopper in the drain of the sink, and turned on both taps. After washing his hands and face, he ducked his head and rinsed his hair. The water

comforted his skin. But the memories of Flo were as tormenting as a fresh burn. Again and again he saw her—the way she'd looked the last time. "By God, Smitty, I hope you roast in Hell."

Back to work, Nels cut electrical tape. To try to take his mind off other things, he sang the song that came first to mind—a parody of the Doxology that he'd learned in childhood. Why that one, he wondered. Was he blaming God?

"Good Morning.

Have you tried Pear's soap?

Hill's Monkey Brand is just the thing.

Celery Compound cures all my ills.

Use Carter's little liver pills.

Sa-po-lee-o!"

Someone called his name. He looked down at Corinna's sweaty face. "Now what?" he asked.

"Miz Haskell. . ."

"She's got our best fan. You're helping her pack. Does she really need me?" He eased wires through the hole behind the dangling kitchen lamp. The large white globe needed a wash, but he had no plans to do it today.

"She's with Miz Weigmann. In the drawin' room." Corinna sounded out of breath. "But Miz Haskell ain't herself. Best you come quick."

Nels climbed down the ladder and lifted his jacket off the door hook. Halfway up the long staircase, he heard the doorbell. "See who it is, Corinna!" he called back.

KALORAMA

The drawing room doors were shut, but he could hear muffled voices. He put on his jacket and pulled up his tie. Then he slid open one of the doors. The room was quite dark. All the draperies were closed against sun and heat.

The women stood well apart near the center of the room. Lois' body looked lost inside an expensive black dress. When he got closer, Nels saw Mid's face and throat had been scratched. He reached out for her, but Lois ran straight at him. Her eyes had the glitter of fever.

Nels caught her small fists. He held her at arm's length so her kicks could not reach him. Dilated pupils made her blue eyes look black. "You took him in. It's your fault! Both of you…" Her mouth contorted as she began to cry. When Nels relaxed his grip, she covered her face with her hands. Mid led her to the nearest chair.

Nels felt someone touch his shoulder. He turned and saw a perspiring gentleman in a custom-tailored, white linen suit. "Senator Shepard! I didn't know you were here."

"You have my apology, Nels. I should have kept her home today. The packing could have waited until Lillian got around to it. She's in Boston arranging for the child's funeral." The senator took a handkerchief from his breast pocket and wiped his forehead. "I've never learned what to do at times like this. I pray and keep going. Almighty God finds ways to help."

He went over to his niece. "My dear child, let's go home." He helped her to stand. As soon as he'd put his arm around her, Lois pressed her face against him. Slowly they made their way to the front door.

Nels and Mid followed. They watched until the pair disappeared inside the Rolls Royce.

"I've got to sit down." Mid went back to the drawing room.

Nels carried the luggage to the porch and locked the door. Then he went to find her. Mid had opened one pair of drapes. She sat on the sofa facing Kalorama Road.

"Antiseptic?" he asked.

She touched the seat beside her. "I need to talk."

They had a clear view of the senator's limousine. The chauffeur was a young colored man in black livery. He moved fast, but it took him several minutes to get all the leather suitcases into the trunk of the car.

"The funeral's Friday. Lois said we're not wanted." Mid gave way to sobs.

Nels wished that he could cry. Flo naked...the odor of urine and semen...her cold, smooth body as he'd searched for a heartbeat.

He put his handkerchief in Mid's lap. "Lois was not much of a mother. Most of the time, she didn't know where Flo was, but to save her soul, she'll never admit it."

"She says you must have suspected that Smitty was…"

"And put my own child in danger?"

"Not one iota of suspicion? You've known him…"

"Seventeen years. Ever since they carted us into Walter Reed." Nels got up and shook his left foot. He stamped it several times. "Even when they decided to take off his arm, he never yelped."

Nels chose an armchair with a hassock and elevated both legs. "One bird on our ward bellyached all the time. Nobody knew why. He looked okay—nothing missing. The whining got on our nerves until Smitty came up with a joke. 'It's a bad case of flying dandruff! Let the poor lad enjoy his misery.' Smitty was a great guy. I don't know why he changed."

Mid glanced at her wristwatch. "Heavens! I've got to wash up and fix us a bite to eat."

She was stopped at the door by Bobbie McElroy.

"Am I glad to be home!" she said. Bobbie piled her bundles on the parlor table, then her white gloves, handbag, and hat. "It's deliciously cool in here. You have no idea how hot it is downtown." She searched through her bundles until she found a package of sheet music and stored it inside the piano bench.

Mid had followed her. "Where's Nora?"

"In the kitchen. Corinna's fixing her a bite to eat. About an hour ago, we had salads and ice cream sodas. Not filling enough, I guess."

"Brood and eat...that's all Nora does these days."

Nels had joined them. "She's searching for comfort."

"What she'll get is fat." Mid frowned. "I'm putting a stop to it right now!"

Bobbie grabbed her arm. "Wait a minute. I have something to tell you."

Mid and Nels exchanged glances. "You bet," he said and led the way to several easy chairs.

Bobbie lit a cigarette. "I'm really worried about Nora. We went to Campbell's summer sale. Sheet music going for half price! Nora didn't care what I picked out for her. All morning she's been...a stranger."

"She has nightmares every night," Mid said. "She suspects we know something we're not telling her."

"We decided to keep it simple," Nels said. "When she asks, we tell her that Flo's with her family."

Bobbie reached for an ashtray and stabbed out her half-smoked cigarette. "Didn't you see the newspaper? We're in the local news. It's all there...everything except why he did it. Nora's bound to find out."

Mid's eyes widened. "No, she won't. We're not going to let her." She gingerly touched her scratches. "Lois blames us."

"She scratched you? How could she! Both of you have been so good to Flo." Bobbie went over to Mid and hugged her.

"Thanks, Bobbie. I really needed that. Nels, lunch in half an hour?"

He nodded. "Go easy on Nora. Food's what she needs right now. Not one of your diet talks. Okay, Mid?"

At the door she turned and looked at him. Against the delicate texture of her skin, the scratches looked jagged and red. She left without answering.

Nels groaned. "My family's hurting. I go right ahead and make matters worse. What's wrong with me? Why can't I see what to do about Nora?"

"Maybe I can help." Bobbie moved to the chair closest to him. "Tomorrow I'm to pick up my train reservations. This time I treated myself to a stateroom. Nora could go with me. She'd love Guadalajara."

Nels kissed her on both cheeks. "More to the point, she'd be away from here. But aren't you just about to leave?"

"Barely enough time to get her ready."

"You'll be gone…"

"Back to the job in a month. Other than that, how long we stayed would be up to Nora." Suddenly Bobbie smiled. "My brother has a little dog. Yappo. Oh, Nels, she could have such a good time!"

KALORAMA

Nels had been observing the changes in her expression. The smile made Bobbie look younger...almost girlish, he thought. "A month in Mexico. Bill will see this as the answer to a prayer. But what will Mid say?"

"She won't let Nora go?"

"Mid thinks the world of you, Bobbie. But the child's never been away from home. Give us a little while to mull it over. Until dinner time?"

"I'll be early."

Mid and her father were having lunch at the kitchen table. As soon as Nels joined them, she handed him a tall glass of iced tea.

"Did the detectives find you?" she asked.

"No, what did they want?"

"They showed us a copy of Smitty's confession."

Bill helped himself to crackers and a wedge of cheese. "He's sworn that he was solely responsible. Criminal assault and suffocation." He reached for the bowl of salad.

"A ten-minute visit at most," Mid said. "They asked if we had anything to bring to their attention. We said no. And they wanted to know where you were. Pop told them."

"So the case is closed?" Nels asked.

Mid shrugged. "No trial date as yet. This thing's far from over. So what do we do about Nora?"

"Where is she now?" Nels asked.

"In Esther's room." Bill said. "They're reading Rachel Field's new book." He smiled. "Nora's keeping me abreast of the story. It's about a wooden doll named Hitty."

"Who has guard duty after that?"

"I guess it's me," Mid said. "Pop's due back at the hospital to sit with Eddie. I'll see to her bath. And a lie-down … at least an hour. Nels, can you stick with her after that?"

"Like her Siamese twin. But what about tomorrow? And every day after that? Bobbie's come up with a plan. She's offering to take Nora to Guadalajara." Nels went to the desk for cigarettes.

"For how long?" Mid asked.

"If Nora's happy, they'll be gone about a month." Nels offered his Old Golds.

Bill tapped a cigarette from the pack. "Bobbie to the rescue! I'll pay the child's train fares."

"Thanks, Pop…and I'll certainly thank Bobbie. But you're going too fast for me. What about Bobbie's crazy brother? What's his name?"

"Lester," Nels said. "He's sick, but he's a good egg. No reason to worry about Lester."

"I go along with Nels," Bill said. "And Jim Hurley is on duty. Lester's in capable hands."

"A couple months ago, Hurley came to the house," Mid said. "Good looking in a muscular sort of way. Was that when you met him?"

"No, Nels and I met him at St. Elizabeth's.

Don't you remember? Bobbie asked us to check him out. We had a number of visits with Lester and Jim."

Nels nodded. "We got acquainted with Jim before Bobbie did. He's a smart cookie. Lester's lucky in some ways."

Mid began to clear the table. "I'd trust Bobbie anywhere. She loves Nora, and Nora loves her. But a whole month so far away?" She turned toward the sink, but Nels had already seen the glint of tears in her eyes.

"What else can we do?" he asked. "Keep the child indoors all summer? She'd go stir crazy. So would we."

Bill went over to his daughter and took her hand. "If Nora stays home, she's bound to hear gossip. Or news on the radio. I'm not sure that she would ever get over it. Bobbie's offer is a godsend." When Bill looked away, Nels saw his anguish. Mid saw it, too, he thought.

Her eyes filled with tears. "You've said that before. A godsend is what you called Flo."

Nels took his wife into his arms. "Sweetheart, we don't have much time. Bobbie gets her reservations tomorrow. She has to hear from us tonight."

As Nels gently dried the scratches, pink spots of Mercurochrome and tears appeared on his white linen handkerchief. Mid stood quietly and tilted her face to help him. He gently kissed her eyes and mouth.

She kissed him back. "You and Pop have your minds made up," she said, "but I've got to be by myself and think."

Nels sighed. "I'll go along with your decision. If you can't bear to let Nora go, she'll stay home. God help us, we'll have to tell her about Flo."

AUGUST

18

By eight-thirty in the morning, Mid was alone in the kitchen. She rinsed her sweaty face, neck, and arms, dried them on the roller towel, and pulled the tortoise shell pins from her curly red hair. She tucked everything into a big ball at the crown of her head. Tendrils escaping the hairpins framed her face in damp ringlets.

Last night's rainfall had not improved the weather. The first week of August was turning out to be as hot and humid as July. Today would be another scorcher, so the sensible thing to do was postpone her trip to town. When the weather cooled, she'd shop for Nora's school things. Today

she'd do something for herself. She sat at the kitchen table to rest and consider what it might be.

For weeks she'd been avoiding mirrors. Now it was time to face the truth. She looked a mess. The tragedy had hit her hard—like some awful illness. For a while she hadn't been able to eat or sleep or care about anything. Even now, it was hard work to keep Flo out of her thoughts. Certain images—the small, nude body in the dumbwaiter—could still trigger an outburst of tears or, far worse, nightmares.

She'd lost over twenty pounds. Every garment she owned was too large, but she was in no mood today to start alterations. Or pound the pavements searching for something stylish and affordable. How ironic! Not long ago, she'd have loved making the most of a new figure.

Nels did not appear to have changed at all. He looked and acted the same as usual. Only she knew the truth about him. Not far beneath the surface were pain and fear. Sometimes they kept him awake, no matter how exhausted he was. As early as four in the morning, he'd be dressed for the day and working on the accounts.

It was time to go upstairs to the meeting he'd called. She got up carefully because the skin of her forearms felt glued to the tabletop. She washed and dried her hands and arms again and tightened the pins in her hair.

Pop was already waiting in the drawing room. He sat in an armchair near the open doors. "I

ought not be here. I'm needed at the hospital," he said.

Mid realized that she'd been staring at her father. He'd shaved and brushed his hair, but his trousers and shirt looked as though he'd slept in them. "I wonder what's keeping Nels," she said.

"He's showing Smitty's suite. The fellow with the British accent came again. What's up, Mid? Why call a meeting?"

"Last night Corinna told us that she's leaving. The Watts are moving back home to Virginia."

"Why? When do they go?"

"A new plant in Suffolk is hiring. Processing peanuts. They both got good jobs. Pop, I hope you'll back me in this meeting. What I want us to do..." But Nels had joined them. He waved a check and smiled.

"The British fellow?" Bill asked.

"He works at the British Legation."

"Does he have a wife?" Mid asked.

"His name is John Stevens, and he's a widower with a nine-year-old son."

Mid frowned. "A boy in the house? I don't know if I'll like that."

"What do you have against boys? He's called Freddy, and we won't see a lot of him. Mostly weekends and vacations. He attends a residential school in Maryland."

"Another child tenant? Why didn't we discuss this?" Mid's face, flushed from the heat, got redder.

Bill glanced at his wristwatch. "It's a done deal; Nels has accepted the check. Look at it this way, Mid. We've filled one expensive vacancy. Now what else must we decide this morning?"

"In a few weeks the Watts are going home to Virginia," Nels said. "Mid and I don't see eye-to-eye about how to replace Corinna."

"You'll never find another Corinna," Bill said.

"Nels has already answered an ad in the *Morning Star*, but I don't..."

Nels interrupted her. "A couple—housekeeper and handyman—will be here for an interview in about twenty minutes. They'd be willing to work for room, board, and not a whole lot more money than we were paying Corinna."

"Do we really need a handyman?" Bill asked.

Mid gave her husband a big grin. "Pop's asking the right question. Maybe you can give him a better answer than you gave me."

"It's a matter of economics," Nels said. "We have to find ways to make more money. If this man is as smart as he sounds, he can make the repairs that eat up my time. I'd work on jobs to improve our income."

"The apartment over the carriage house?" Bill asked.

"All it needs is a heating system, and I know what to do. All I need is time to install it."

"What about Fourth Floor?" Bill asked. "A couple years ago you wanted to convert those single rooms into larger units."

"I'm still interested. The snag there is the cost of putting in an elevator."

"Bank loan? Second mortgage?" Bill suggested.

Mid got up from her chair. "You're scaring me. I'll see you in a few minutes...after I do something about my hair." She was pulling out the pins as she headed toward her bathroom.

She used a cool, wet washrag on all her exposed skin and combed through her hair with her favorite broad-toothed comb. Once again she secured the ball of curls on top of her head. Before leaving the bathroom she washed her handkerchief and smoothed it against the mirror on the medicine cabinet. She spread the linen square so it would dry without a wrinkle.

In the bedroom she sprinkled a few drops of Lily of The Valley cologne on a fresh handkerchief and slipped it into the pocket of her jumper.

The men stood near the front door. She could tell from their smiles and handshake that they had reached some kind of agreement.

"Nels is on the right track," her father said. "We can afford to hire this couple. If you like both of them, why not offer them a month's trial?" After a quick kiss on her forehead, he hurried out the door.

"I'm going to Fourth Floor," Nels said. "There's something I need to check. Want to come along?"

He was smiling at her, but she did not smile back. They've agreed on everything, she thought, and without talking it over with me. "No thanks," she said. "I need to call the beauty parlor and make an appointment."

No matter what Pop thought, no matter what Nels said, she had put up with her "crowning glory" long enough. The time had come to cut her hair.

19

At last, Nels had gone back to sleep. Their brief talk was what he'd needed. What she needed was a hot drink. And to get over feeling ashamed of herself. She eased out of the bed and into her dressing gown and slippers.

Before Mid reached the kitchen, she smelled hot chocolate.

"Well, hello, Curly Top! Want some cocoa?" her father asked. At her nod, he filled two cups and carried them to the table.

"A hot drink always helps," she said.

"I can't sleep either."

At two in the morning, the kitchen was about as cool as it would be all day. Only the wall lamp above the stove was lit, but she could see gray bags under her father's eyes. He looked almost as worn

out as his seersucker robe. "What's keeping you awake?" she asked. "Uncle Eddie? I went to see him today, but he wasn't up to a visit."

"Some nurse forgot him. When I'm there, I make damn sure he gets his morphine on time."

"You're there a lot."

"I'd stay 'round the clock if they'd let me." He went to the stove for the pot of cocoa and shared what was left. "Eddie's always on my mind. What about you? Still worrying about Nora?"

"Not since we got the wire from Bobbie. And Nora's postcards. Aren't they great? But I wish she'd come home."

"Good grief, Mid, don't wish her back too soon! Not while folks are still talking about the murder." He rubbed his face and yawned. "If Nora's not keeping you awake, what is?" He went to get a cigarette. Nels always kept a few packs in the desk.

How much should she tell? That she'd been awakened by the sound of Nels crying? She didn't know all the reasons, but the little she'd coaxed out of him had hurt. Should she hand Pop his fair share of guilt?

Pop was giving most of his time to Eddie. The only service he gave Kalorama was at meal time. He'd been leaving his other jobs for Nels to do. Since the murder she'd been leaning on Nels, too. She'd been babying herself, catering to sick headaches and bad nerves. Nels had been taking it

on the chin. But not anymore. Starting today, she'd be back on the job full time.

"I've been a bad girl, Pop. A slacker. Believe it or not, I still haven't written to Letty. All I've done so far is address the envelope and waste a lot of stationery. Nels can't understand why I'm having so much trouble. He says, 'Tell her the facts. Leave out the mush.'"

"He's right, Mid. If you get it done today, I'll post the letter on my way to the hospital." He dropped the butt of his cigarette in the ashtray and reached for her empty cup.

"The dishes are my job, Pop."

"That's my good girl!" He kissed the top of her head.

She listened as he dragged his slippered feet along the hall carpet. At the click of his door latch, she got up to take the dishes to the sink and return the pack of Old Golds to the desk. It took nearly an hour to compose and copy the letter.

Dear Letty,

I wish I had no reason to send you this painful news. Flo is dead. Smitty is in jail.
This is what happened—as far as we know. Flo was on her own. Lois was sick in bed, and Nora was at the movie matinee. At about two o'clock, Flo went to see Esther. After a brief

visit, the child wandered around the neighborhood and the house. At some point she went up to Fourth Floor. Apparently she sometimes went there to skate.

That afternoon she discovered the service staircase. It goes from Fourth Floor to First and ends in Smitty's back hall. He was surprised to find her there, looking sweaty and dirty after her climb down the stairs. Smitty claims that she asked him to help her clean up. The washing led to fondling. Smitty says that Flo liked being tickled and kissed. He lost control of himself—blamed the bourbon highballs he'd had during that afternoon.

Flo ran away from him and was crying and banging on Nora's bedroom door when he caught her. At that same time, some people on Second Floor were starting down the stairs. Smitty says that he only wanted to silence the child. Handicapped as he is, and in his haste to shut her up, he suffocated her. No one saw him do it. No one saw him hide her body in the dumbwaiter.

To appear innocent of the crime, he intended to spend that evening as he did every Saturday —dinner followed by bridge. He went down to the dining hall. Walt and Esther, who sat near him, described him as untidy and intoxicated. They said he seemed stunned when the police

arrived. At the police station Smitty broke down and confessed.

Please tell Janet.

Love,
Mid

20

There were no vehicles in front of 1867 Kalorama Road. Nels parked in his favorite spot. He was about to get out of the car when a sharp pain stopped him. He rubbed his leg until the pain became a familiar buzz. What it needed was elevation. Could he afford the time? He'd promised to get right back to the funeral home. With Bill's lunch. Bill wouldn't leave Eddie. For fifteen hours he'd sat with the body of his best friend.

Nels eased himself out of the car and reached into the back seat for the dry cleaning. Aristo had done a nifty job on his dark suit. The shine was gone. Mid would be wearing a brand new outfit. Her old black dress was too big. "Besides, it's for Eddie," she'd explained. Nels sighed. $10.95 for a

black jersey dress. Twenty bucks for the hat! Black satin and felt with a squared-off brim. Eddie wouldn't know what she wore, and Bill wouldn't care. All that mattered to them were the folks from the old neighborhood. Nels muttered, "I hope to God some of them show up tomorrow."

Slowly he climbed the sixteen steps to the front door and let himself into the entrance hall. Corinna looked up from sorting the mail. On the hall table short stacks of envelopes surrounded a jardinière of yellow, orange, and red daylilies. "You got two picture postcards," she said. Her dimple appeared. How good it was to see her smile again!

He scanned the cards. "I'll take 'em downstairs in a few minutes. I have to unload the dry cleaning."

In the bedroom, he hung his suit in the wardrobe. Nora's school clothes? Mid would want to inspect them. He draped them over the back of the loveseat. He rested on the bedside chair and studied the messages on the cards. Cheery, even between the lines. He unlaced his shoes and lifted both legs onto the bed.

There was something wrong with the chairs at funeral parlors. They weren't designed for long waits. The fancy place in Arm Arbor had been uncomfortable, too. He and Mid had spent an afternoon and evening with the body of his father. They'd gone through the expected motions—giving and receiving hushed greetings. What else was there to do? He had no memories of his mother,

who had died when he was two. There were no warm memories of his father. The hardworking lawyer had devoted himself to his clients and given little time to his son. A dozen visitors, mostly neighbors, came to the funeral parlor. More than twenty attended the funeral, but only eleven bothered to sign the book at the church. Nels did not recognize all the names.

Despite an organist and flowers, the sanctuary was as awesome and chilly as ever. The young pastor who performed the service mispronounced their name. Before Nels could decide what to do, the brief ceremony was over. Would his father have corrected the pastor? He didn't know.

For himself, be wanted none of it. No casket, no ritual, no grave. His ashes would come here—to the rose garden. He reached under the edge of the bed for his old shoes.

The kitchen smelled of fresh bread and cake. He kissed the nape of Mid's neck and waved the cards. "Which one first?"

Mid did not look up. She was pouring glaze over a large sheet cake. "Guadalajara. Who wrote this one?" She got two cups and the percolator and joined him at the table.

"Nora's telling about a fiesta. She ate too many carne tacos. Yappo did, too." He handed her the

card. A local artist had sketched a resplendent bougainvillea vine.

"Home in less than two weeks," he said. "But Letty says she can't get back until October. She's bought a townhouse." He put his legs across the seat of the next chair.

"Any news of Janet?"

"She and the child love their new home. And Paris."

"First a boutique and now a townhouse. Fancy that!" Mid studied the picture of L'Arc de Triomphe.

"We got to the funeral parlor before the doors were open. No breakfast this morning."

She poured coffee and brought him a box of saltines. "Many viewers?"

"Lots. Everyone's surprised to see how well Eddie looks. I don't think I ever saw him in a suit. I miss the clean apron. And his smile."

She served him split pea soup and pie. "Pop loves fresh peach. I'll send him a big piece. Did he tell you what he wants for his lunch?"

"The only food he talked about was the spread for tomorrow. He's afraid of running out."

"How many are coming?"

"Maybe twenty. Not counting us. Did you invite the Menafees?"

"Edith said yes."

"Good! Bill will like that."

"He wanted us to pick crabs. Can you picture that? Twenty mourners picking crabs?" Nels

laughed. "He said you'd settled on salads, including crab salad."

She nodded. "We compromised on the beverages, too. Iced tea and one keg of beer." "Eddie'd go along with that. Buffet at one o'clock?"

"I don't know. Some may linger at the cemetery."

"No reason to rush. Whenever folks get here, I'll steer 'em into the drawing room. They can rest and chin until Bill decides it's time to eat."

She collected the dishes and set them in the dishpan. "Have you seen the *Morning Star*?"

"No, did they run the right ad?"

"The one you wanted, but you'll have to change it. A whole lot happened this morning. Take a look at this." She searched through the newspaper before she handed it to him.

VETERAN COMMITTED

Hamilton Balfour Smith III, 59, was yesterday committed to St. Elizabeth's Asylum by order of Judge Hugo Bolwell. Col. Smith, decorated veteran of the Spanish-American War and Great War, has been on trial for the criminal assault and suffocation of Florence Louisa Haskell, 6.

"Not one word about Kalorama," Mid said.

"Good. But what about Smitty? The day I took his mail to him, I couldn't make sense of anything he said."

"All I know is that his nephew called. The movers are coming for his things on Monday afternoon. Stevens can move in on…Wednesday."

"But how does that change the ad?"

"That's not all. Hang onto your hat! We've rented the Haskells' suite."

"Hallelujah! Tell me about our new boarders."

Mid didn't answer. She's waiting for me to taste the pie, he thought. He took a big bite and threw her a kiss.

"Esther and Walt want it. They're getting married! You should have seen 'em. Like excited kids!"

Nels grinned at her. "Good for Walt. He's decided to make an honest woman of her."

"What on earth do you mean?"

"Come off it, Mid. You know they've been sleeping together. For months."

"No time for such talk. Pop's waiting for his lunch. While I fix it, how about writing our new ad? I could call it in this afternoon. The only vacancies are two singles on the third floor."

On his way to the desk, Nels turned on the radio. He searched the dial until he found an orchestra playing a medley of songs from the new musical, "Roberta". Then came a sing-a-long of old favorites. The radio voices were strong and lively. Soon Nels was singing with them.

Mid kept working, but she sang, too.

"Grab your coat and get your hat,

KALORAMA

Leave your troubles on the doorstep.
Life can be so sweet
On the sunny side of the street."

LaVergne, TN USA
10 January 2011
211866LV00001B/72/A